THE BIRDS AND BEASTS OF MARK TWAIN

THE
BIRDS
AND
BEASTS
OF
MARK
TWAIN

Edited by Robert M. Rodney
and Minnie M. Brashear

Original paintings and drawings by
Robert Roché

UNIVERSITY OF OKLAHOMA PRESS : NORMAN

Acknowledgment is hereby made for permission most generously given by Harper & Row, publishers, and the Samuel Langhorne Clemens estate to quote from the following published works by Mark Twain:

"Jim Wolf and the Cats" (I, 135-38) and the cat vignette by Susie Clemens (II, 82) from *Mark Twain's Autobiography* (copyright 1924 by Clara Gabrilowitsch; renewed 1952 by Clara Clemens Samossoud); Letter to Mrs. Mabel Patterson, in Chicago, Oct. 2, 1908, from *Mark Twain's Letters*, II, 821 (copyright 1917 by Mark Twain Company; renewed 1945 by Clara Clemens Samossoud); "A Horse's Tale" from *The Mysterious Stranger and Other Stories* (copyright 1906 by Harper & Brothers).

Samuel Clemens' letter to Annie Taylor from "Letters Mark Twain Wrote in 1857," Kansas City *Star Magazine,* March 21, 1926, is reprinted by permission of the Kansas City *Star.*

Library of Congress Catalog Card Number 66-22718

ISBN: 978-0-8061-1120-9 (paper)

The paper in this book meets the guidelines for permanence and durability of the Committee on Production Guidelines for Book Longevity of the Council of Library Resources, Inc.

Copyright © 1966 by the University of Oklahoma Press, Norman, Publishing Division of the University. Manufactured in the U.S.A. Paperback edition published 1973.

TO MY WIFE ISOBEL
AND TO THE LATE M. M. BRASHEAR
FOR THEIR SUSTAINED ENTHUSIASM
AND ENCOURAGEMENT

FOREWORD

MARK TWAIN has been a perennial favorite of readers of all ages for almost a century now. He has been obscured frequently in the national vision by wars, national elections, atomic energy, television, space exploration, and other distractions of the twentieth century that would have diverted the humorist himself. But he always re-emerges to capture again our imaginations with his portrayals of the American past, his refreshing observations of the world at large, and his human insights. As long as there are literate audiences at home and abroad, such books as *Roughing It, The Adventures of Huckleberry Finn, Life on the Mississippi,* and *A Connecticut Yankee in King Arthur's Court* will be a vital part of the human experience.

Mark Twain's range and variety of interests, the fluency and naturalness of his style, and his buoyant spirit appeal to both the young and the old. In certain respects young readers are even better equipped to enjoy Mark Twain because of their flexible literary tastes and their delighted response to anything that is fresh and original. But they can respond only if what most appeals to them in a writer of this kind can be readily found. Unfortunately, many of Mark Twain's best stories, anecdotes, and sketches are widely scattered among his many books, often imbedded in long, prosaic stretches of his travel accounts, where they are inaccessible to all but the most thorough-going reader. The editors of the present book believe that if newer generations of readers are to become acquainted with this most American of writers, he will have to be introduced to them in collections of this kind.

What appeals most strongly to the modern urban reader is Mark Twain's depiction of the natural world: rural Missouri, the Mississippi, the Great Plains, grandeurs of the American West, the sea, the picturesque landscapes of Europe, the wonders of the South Pacific, of Asia, and of Africa. From the exhilaration of his earliest experiences through the disillusioned and embittered reflections of his latest years, this writer retained his youthful enthusiasm for the natural world and zest for adventuring into strange and far-away places.

It has been seldom noted that Mark Twain had a wide-ranging curiosity about animals. From the lowly frog of California to the proud elephant of India, he found grist for his mill in fauna of all kinds. In America he wrote sketches of the horses, the buffaloes, and coyotes and other wild creatures of the West, as well as cats and other domestic acquaintances. While abroad, he recorded his impressions of the kangaroo, the ornithorhyncus, and other exotics of Australasia; the monkeys, the elephants, and the crows of India; the omnivorous camel of the Middle East. In Europe he made notes for later stories and sketches, taking special delight in the antics of ravens and ants that he encountered in the Black Forest of Germany. Even the sharks and porpoises of the sea came under his close scrutiny. The reader's interest in these sketches may center in Mark Twain's perception of human traits in these birds and beasts and the caricature and satire of his portraits, but just as frequently the reader may appreciate his description of the sheer beauty of animal form and movement. Or it may be the natural and unconscious dignity that he reveals in animal behavior. A close reading of the travel books turns up more than fifty land and sea creatures in *Roughing It, A Tramp Abroad*, and *Following the Equator*—besides the special animals that inspired some of Mark Twain's best yarns and anecdotes. Not all of these creatures became famous enough to promote such celebrations as the annual frog jumping contest in California, but the pen of the great humorist has made all of them memorable.

In our time, Walt Disney and his fellow artists have made a unique contribution to comic entertainment through their animated animal cartoons. Long before these craftsmen, however, a fascinating animal world was revealed to Victorian readers. Through the craft of words a unique writer gave them delightful portraits done with a mixture of scientific accuracy, caricature, pathos, and humor. The editors hope that this book will enable present-day readers, both young and old, to enjoy that world with Mark Twain.

R. M. RODNEY
M. M. BRASHEAR

ABOUT THE ARTIST

APPRENTICED at the age of ten in the studio of the Spanish portrait painter Sebastian Cruset, Robert Roché, two years later, was the youngest person ever to be enrolled in the National Academy of Design. He studied under such leading painters as Charles Louis Hinton, Sidney Dickinson, George B. Bridgeman, Henry Rittenberg, and William C. Palmer. He continued his studies at the Art Students League and ended his formal training with several years of anatomical research.

This unusual background eminently equipped Mr. Roché to work in all media and with a great variety of subject matter. The range of his technique is remarkable: he can go from the most minute, detailed linear work to the freest type of painting. With the added gift of being able to adapt his technical approach to any subject at hand, he can evoke the quality and mood of whatever he is working on. If he has a specialty, it is perhaps best reflected in his character portraits of people and animals. In the opinion of many experts, his action paintings of horses are in a class by themselves, and he is without a peer in his studies and interpretations of animal character and behavior. This combination of talents made him an inevitable choice to portray the birds and beasts of Mark Twain. A freelance artist rather than an illustrator, Mr. Roché readily consented to this particular assignment because of his life-long enthusiasm for Mark Twain as well as his love of animals. Each of the portraits in this book is the product of painstaking preliminary research, during which he spent six weeks studying real-life bullfrogs alone, together with many other weeks observing captive specimens of Mark Twain's other animalia, before he set up his easel.

Mr. Roché has won some forty first prizes at regional and national exhibitions and is represented in many public collections—the Goodyear, the Jackson, the Tobias, and the Kellogg, to name but some—as well as in many private collections. Since he opened his first working studio in New York at the age of seventeen, he has had sixty-five one-man shows in the United States, including two large New York shows at the Frank K. M. Rehn Galleries.

When the New York Racing Association commissioned an artist for the first time in its distinguished history, Mr. Roché was chosen to produce the celebrated half-life-size portrait of the famous race horse Man o' War. In addition, he has painted a series of the Old Saratoga Race Track and a series of the Belmont Track for the N.Y.R.A. For several years he has been executing a series of oil portraits of famous Americans. Painted from life, they are destined to be hung in the Capitol Building in Washington. Completed thus far are his studies of Harry S Truman, Eleanor Roosevelt, Bernard Baruch, and Dr. Ralph Bunche.

Robert Roché and his wife live near New Durham, New Hampshire, in a 1772 farmhouse, perfectly restored by their own hands. He paints in an adjoining studio, interrupting his daily work long enough to tend to his livestock and exercise his bird dogs.

CONTENTS

4 · SOME ANIMAL TALES

THE BIRDS AND BEASTS OF MARK TWAIN

1 · DOMESTICS

*As early as 1857, long before he wrote his "Celebrated Jump-
ing Frog" story and books embodying animal portraits, Mark
Twain revealed a flair for writing fables. Corresponding with
a girl friend while he was working in his brother Orion's job-
printing office in Keokuk, Iowa, young Samuel Clemens
entertained her with a short description of a congregation of
insects attracted to his lamp, in the midst of whom he visual-
ized himself as a sort of Gulliver:*

3

Bugs! Yes, B-U-G-S! What of the bugs? Why, perdition take the bugs! That is all. Night before last I stood at the little press until nearly 2 o'clock, and the flaring gas light over my head attracted all the varieties of bugs which are to be found in natural history, and they all had the same praise-worthy recklessness about flying into the fire. They at first came in little social crowds of a dozen or so, but soon increased in numbers, until a religious meeting of several millions was assembled on the board before me, presided over by a venerable beetle, who occupied the most prominent lock of my hair as his chair of state, while innumerable lesser dignitaries of the same tribe were clustered around him, keeping order, and at the same time endeavoring to attract the attention of the vast assemblage to their own importance by industriously grating their teeth. It must have been an interesting occasion —perhaps a great bug jubilee commemorating the triumph of the locusts over Pharaoh's crops in Egypt many centuries ago. . . .

The big "president" beetle (who, when he frowned, closely resembled Isbell when the pupils are out of time) rose and ducked his head and, crossing his arms over his shoulders, stroked them down to the tip of his nose several times, and after thus disposing of the perspiration, stuck his hands under his wings, propped his back against a lock of hair, and then, bobbing his head at the congregation, remarked, "B-u-z-z!" To which the congregation devoutly responded, "B-u-z-z!" Satisfied with this promptness on the part of his flock, he took a more imposing perpendicular against another lock of hair and, lifting his hands to command silence, gave another melodious "b-u-z-z!" on a louder key (which I suppose to have

4

been the key-note) and after a moment's silence the whole congregation burst into a grand anthem, three dignified daddy longlegs, perched near the gas burner, beating quadruple time during the performance. Soon two of the parts in the great chorus maintained silence, while a treble and alto duet, sung by forty-seven thousand mosquitoes and twenty-three thousand house flies, came in, and then, after another chorus, a tenor and bass duet by thirty-two thousand locusts and ninety-seven thousand pinch bugs was sung—then another grand chorus, "Let Every Bug Rejoice and Sing" (we used to sing "heart" instead of "bug") terminated the performance, during which eleven treble singers split their throats from head to heels, and the patriotic "daddies" who beat time hadn't a stump of a leg left. (Letter to Annie Taylor, first published in the Kansas City *Star Magazine*, Sunday, March 21, 1926.)

Mark Twain's interest in domestic fauna, however, is better illustrated by his observations on cats. During most of his life he surrounded himself with whole housefuls of cats, not to keep rodents away, but rather to indulge his fondness for kittens and to delight in the older cats' graceful movements and their lazy enjoyment of domestic comfort. As a boy he had always owned a cat, and it generally had a seat beside him at the table. There were cats at his Aunt Patsie Quarles's Quarry Farm, where he spent his summers; and they were an inevitable décor of his own later homes in Hartford and Redding, Connecticut. Mark Twain's little daughter Susy revealed in her "biography" of her father written when she was thirteen years old:

5

Papa is very fond of animals, particularly of cats. We had a dear little gray kitten once that he named "Lazy" (papa always wears gray to match his hair and eyes) and he would carry him around on his shoulder, it was a mighty pretty sight! the gray cat sound asleep against papa's gray coat and hair. The names that he has given our different cats, are really remarkably funny, they are namely Stray Kit, Abner, Motley, Fraeulein, Lazy, Buffalo Bill, Soapy Sall, Cleveland, Sour Mash, and Pestilence and Famine.

Mark Twain himself recalls in his Autobiography *how the names of the cats confused his children:*

At one time when the children were small we had a very black mother-cat named Satan, and Satan had a small off-spring named Sin. Pronouns were a difficulty for the children. Little Clara came in one day, her black eyes snapping with indignation, and said: "Papa, Satan ought to be punished. She is out there at the greenhouse and there she stays and stays, and his kitten is downstairs, crying."

In his later and lonelier years at Redding, Mark Twain kept a gray mother cat named Tammany and her kittens, whose capers were his chief delight. In a letter to his Chicago friend Mrs. Patterson, just two years before his death, he wrote:

If I can find a photograph of "Tammany" and her kittens, I will enclose it in this. One of them likes to be crammed into a corner-pocket of the billiard table—which he fits as snugly as does a finger in a glove and then he watches the game (and obstructs it) by the hour, and spoils many a shot by putting out his paw and changing the direction of

6

a passing ball. Whenever a ball is in his arms, or so close to him that it cannot be played without risk of hurting him, the player is privileged to remove it to anyone of the three spots that chances to be vacant.

THE CAT AND THE PAIN-KILLER

The cats that we meet in Mark Twain's stories, however, do not enjoy the affection and comfort of Mark Twain's own household. The kindly satisfaction that the author took in their companionship becomes mirth at the plight of his fictional cats when they are surprised, rather cruelly, out of their calm. In THE ADVENTURES OF TOM SAWYER *(1875), for example, we meet a cat that cures Tom's Aunt Polly of the habit of trying to cure Tom of imaginary illness. When Aunt Polly fails to cure Tom of his love-sickness for Becky Thatcher by giving him hot and cold baths and vigorous scrubbings, she decides to give the boy internal treatment with patent medicines:*

She calculated his capacity as she would a jug's, and filled him up every day with quack cure-alls.

Tom had become indifferent to persecution by this time. This phase filled the old lady's heart with consternation. This indifference must be broken up at any cost. Now she heard of Pain-killer for the first time. She ordered a lot at once. She tasted it and was filled with gratitude. It was simply fire in a liquid form. She dropped the water treatment and everything else, and pinned her faith to Pain-killer. She gave Tom a teaspoonful and watched with the deepest anxiety for the result. Her troubles were instantly at rest, her soul at peace again; for the "indifference" was broken up. The boy could not have shown a wilder, heartier interest if she had built a fire under him.

Tom felt that it was time to wake up; this sort of life might be romantic enough, in this blighted condition, but it was getting to have too little sentiment and too much distracting variety about it. So he thought over various plans for relief, and finally hit upon that of professing to be fond of Pain-killer. He asked for it so often that he became a nuisance, and his aunt ended by telling him to help himself and quit bothering her. If it had been Sid, she would have had no misgivings to alloy her delight; but since it was Tom, she watched the bottle clandestinely. She found that the medicine did really diminish, but it did not occur to her that the boy was mending the health of a crack in the sitting-room floor with it.

One day he was in the act of dosing the crack when his aunt's yellow cat came along, purring, eyeing the teaspoon avariciously, and begging for a taste. Tom said:

"Don't ask for it unless you want it, Peter."

But Peter signified that he did want it.

"You better make sure."

Peter was sure.

"Now you've asked for it, and I'll give it to you, because there ain't anything mean about *me*; but if you find you don't like it, you mustn't blame anybody but your own self."

Peter was agreeable. So Tom pried his mouth open and poured down the Pain-killer. Peter sprang a couple of yards in the air, and then delivered a war-whoop and set off round and round the room, banging against furniture, upsetting flower-pots, and making general havoc. Next he rose on his hind feet and pranced around, in a frenzy of enjoyment, with

8

his head over his shoulder and his voice proclaiming his unappeasable happiness. Then he went tearing around the house again spreading chaos and destruction in his path. Aunt Polly entered in time to see him throw a few double somersets, deliver a final mighty hurrah, and sail through the open window, carrying the rest of the flower-pots with him. The old lady stood petrified with astonishment, peering over her glasses; Tom lay on the floor expiring with laughter.

Enough of this episode.

If the reader wants to find out what happens between Tom and Aunt Polly at this point, all that he needs to do is go to chapter twelve of Tom Sawyer. (*The picture of the cat is complete.*)

JIM WOLF AND THE CATS

In his Autobiography (*1924*) *Mark Twain retells a cat story which was probably the first story he ever published and one which was often stolen from him. Although the story is more about the cruel plight of his trusting boyhood friend, whom he lured into disgrace, it is two "sentimental cats" on a moonlight night that help the "villain" to carry out his dastardly deed:*

It was back in those far-distant days—1848 or '49—that Jim Wolf came to us. He was from a hamlet thirty or forty miles back in the country, and he brought all his native sweetnesses and gentlenesses and simplicities with him. He was approaching seventeen, a grave and slender lad, trustful, honest, honorable, a creature to love and cling to. And he was incredibly bashful. He was with us a good while, but he could never conquer that peculiarity; he could not be at ease in the presence of any woman, not even in my good and gentle mother's; and as to speaking to any girl, it was wholly impossible. He sat perfectly still, one day—there were ladies chatting in the room—while a wasp up his leg stabbed him cruelly a dozen times; and all the sign he gave was a slight wince for each stab and the tear of torture in his eye. He was too bashful to move.

It is to this kind that untoward things happen. My sister gave a "candy-pull" on a winter's night. I was too young to be of the company, and Jim was too diffident. I was sent up to bed early, and Jim followed of his own motion. His room was in the new part of the house and his window looked out on the roof of the L annex. That roof was six inches deep in snow, and the snow had an ice crust upon it which was as slick as glass. Out of the comb of the roof projected a short chimney, a common resort for sentimental cats on light nights—and this was a moonlight night. Down at the eaves, below the chimney, a canopy of dead vines spread away to some posts, making a cozy shelter, and after an hour or two the rollicking crowd of young ladies and gentlemen grouped themselves in its shade, with their saucers of liquid and piping-hot candy disposed about them on the frozen ground to cool. There was joyous chaffing and joking and laughter—peal upon peal of it.

About this time a couple of old, disreputable tomcats got up on the chimney and started a heated argument about something; also about this time I gave up trying to get to sleep and went visiting to Jim's room. He was awake and fuming about the cats and their intolerable yowling. I asked him, mockingly, why he didn't climb out and drive them away. He was nettled, and said overboldly that for two cents he *would*.

It was a rash remark and was probably repented of before it was fairly out of his mouth. But it was too late—he was committed. I knew him; and I knew he would rather break his neck than back down, if I egged him on judiciously.

"Oh, of course you would! Who's doubting it?"

It galled him, and he burst out, with sharp irritation, "Maybe *you* doubt it!"

"I? Oh no! I shouldn't think of such a thing. You are always doing wonderful things, with your mouth."

He was in a passion now. He snatched on his yarn socks and began to raise the window, saying in a voice quivering with anger:

"*You* think I dasn't—you do! Think what you blame please. *I* don't care what you think. I'll show you!"

The window made him rage; it wouldn't stay up.

I said, "Never mind, I'll hold it."

Indeed, I would have done anything to help. I was only a boy and was already in a radiant heaven of anticipation. He climbed carefully out, clung to the window sill until his feet were safely placed, then began to pick his perilous way on all-fours along the glassy comb, a foot and a hand on each side of it. I believe I enjoy it now as much as I did then; yet it is nearly fifty years ago. The frosty breeze flapped his short shirt about his lean legs; the crystal roof shone like polished marble in the intense glory of the moon; the unconscious cats sat erect upon the chimney, alertly watching each other, lashing their tails and pouring out their hollow grievances; and slowly and cautiously Jim crept on, flapping as he went, the gay and frolic-some young creatures under the vine canopy unaware, and outraging these solemnities with their misplaced laughter. Every time Jim slipped I had a hope; but always on he crept and disappointed it. At last he was within reaching distance. He paused, raised himself carefully up, measured his distance deliberately, then made a frantic grab at the nearest cat—and missed it. Of course he lost his balance. His heels flew up, he struck on his back, and like a rocket he darted down the roof feet first, crashed through the dead vines, and landed in a sitting position in fourteen saucers of red-hot candy, in the midst of all that party—and dressed as he was—this lad who could not look a girl in the face with his clothes on. There was a wild scramble and a storm of shrieks, and Jim fled up the stairs, dripping broken crockery all the way.

THE POODLE DOG AND THE PINCH BUG

Strictly speaking, a dog is a "carnivorous domesticated mammal," according to the dictionary. If his only interest in life were eating and obeying his master, he might live happily enough. But his great curiosity about everything in general often gets him into trouble, especially in Mark Twain's animal world. Two of the dogs he writes about in his earlier books would be well described by another dictionary definition of dog: "a mean worthless fellow; a wretch."

In The Adventures of Tom Sawyer *Mark Twain relates how a poodle dog disrupted a whole church service by his encounter with a pinch bug:*

There was a rustling of dresses, and the standing congregation sat down. The boy whose history this book relates did not enjoy the prayer, he only endured it . . . In the midst of the prayer a fly had lit on the back of the pew in front of him and tortured his spirit by calmly rubbing its hands together, embracing its head with its arms, and polishing it so vigorously that it seemed to almost part company with the body, and the slender thread of a neck was exposed to view; scraping its wings with its hind legs and smoothing them to its body as if they had been coat-tails; going through its whole toilet as tranquilly as if it knew it was perfectly safe. As indeed it was; for as sorely as Tom's hands itched to grab for it they did not dare—he believed his soul would be instantly destroyed if he did such a thing while the prayer was going on. But with the closing sentence his hand began to curve and steal forward; and the instant the "Amen" was out the fly was a prisoner of war. His aunt detected the act and made him let it go.

The minister gave out his text and droned along monotonously through an argument that was so prosy that many a head by and by began to nod. . . .

Now [Tom] lapsed into suffering again, as the dry argument was resumed. Presently he bethought him of a treasure he had and got it out. It was a large black beetle with formidable jaws—a "pinch bug," he called it. It was in a percussion-cap box. The first thing the beetle did was to take him by the finger. A natural fillip followed, the beetle went floundering into the aisle and lit on its back, and the hurt finger went into the boy's mouth. The beetle lay there working its helpless legs, unable to turn over. Tom eyed it, and longed for it; but it was safe out of his reach. Other people uninterested in the sermon, found relief in the beetle, and they eyed it too. Presently a vagrant poodle-dog came idling along, sad at heart, lazy with the summer softness and the quiet, weary of captivity, sighing for change. He spied the beetle; the drooping tail lifted and wagged. He surveyed the prize; walked around it; smelt at it from a safe distance; walked around it again; grew bolder, and took a closer smell; then lifted his lip and made a gingerly snatch at it, just missing it; made another, and another; began to enjoy the diversion; subsided to his stomach with the beetle between his paws, and continued his experiments; grew weary at last, and then indifferent and absent-minded. His head nodded, and little by little his chin descended and touched the enemy, who seized it. There was a sharp yelp, a flirt of the poodle's head, and the beetle fell a couple of yards away, and lit on its back once more. The neighboring spectators shook with a gentle inward joy, several faces went behind fans and handkerchiefs, and Tom was entirely happy. The dog looked foolish, and probably felt so; but there was resentment in his heart, too, and a craving for revenge. So he went to the beetle and began a wary attack on it again; jumping at it from every point of a circle, lighting with his fore paws within an inch of the creature, making even closer snatches at it with his teeth, and jerking his head till his ears flapped again. But he grew tired once more, after a while; tried to amuse himself with a fly but found no relief; followed an ant around, with his nose close to the floor, and quickly wearied of that; yawned, sighed, forgot the beetle entirely, and sat down on it. Then there was a wild yelp of agony and the poodle went sailing up the aisle; the yelps continued, and so did the dog; he crossed the house in front of the altar; he flew down the other aisle; he crossed before the doors; he clamored up the home-stretch; his anguish grew with his progress, till presently he was but a woolly comet moving in its orbit with the gleam and the speed of light. At last the frantic sufferer sheered from its course, and sprang into its master's lap; he flung it out of the window, and the voice of distress quickly thinned away and died in the distance.

By this time the whole church was red-faced and suffocating with suppressed laughter, and the sermon had come to a dead standstill. . . . It was a genuine relief to the whole congregation when the ordeal was over and the benediction pronounced.

Tom Sawyer went home quite cheerful, thinking to himself that there was some satisfaction about divine service when there was a bit of variety in it. He had but one marring thought; he was willing that the dog should play with his pinch bug, but he did not think it was upright in him to carry it off.

THE DACHSHUND

In Following the Equator, *a travel book of the year 1897, we are presented with the portrait of a dachshund that certainly aroused Mark Twain's curiosity though it did not command his admiration:*

a remarkable looking dog . . . whose coat was smooth and shiny and black, and I think had tan trimmings around the edges and perhaps underneath. It was a long, low dog, with very short, strange legs—legs that curved inboard, something like parentheses turned the wrong way (. Indeed, it was made on the plan of a bench for length and lowness. It seemed to be satisfied, but I thought the plan poor, and structurally weak, on account of the distance between the forward supports and those abaft. With age the dog's back was likely to sag; and it seemed to me that it would have been a stronger and more practicable dog if it had had some more legs. It had not begun to sag yet, but the shape of the legs showed that the undue weight imposed upon them was beginning to tell. It had a long nose, and floppy ears that hung down, and a resigned expression of countenance. I did not like to ask what kind of a dog it was, or how it came to be deformed, for it was plain that the gentleman was very fond of it, and naturally he could be sensitive about it. From delicacy I thought it best not to seem to notice it too much. No doubt a man with a dog like that feels just as a person does who has a child that is out of true. The gentleman was not merely fond of the dog, he was also proud of it—just the same, again, as a mother feels about her child when it is an idiot. I could see that he was proud of it, notwithstanding it was such a long dog and looked so resigned and pious. It had been all over the world with him, and had been pilgriming like that for years and years. It had traveled 50,000 miles by sea and rail, and had ridden in front of him on his horse 8,000. It had a silver medal from the Geographical Society of Great Britain for its travels, and I saw it. It had won prizes in dog shows, both in India and in England—I saw them. He said its pedigree was on record in the Kennel Club, and that it was a well-known dog. He said a great many people in London could recognize it the moment they saw it. I did not say anything, but I did not think it anything strange; I should know that dog again, myself, yet I am not careful about noticing dogs. He said that when he walked along in London, people often stopped and looked at the dog. Of course I did not say anything, for I did not want to hurt his feelings, but I could have explained to him that if you take a great long low dog like that and waddle it along the street anywhere in the world and not charge anything, people will stop and look. He was gratified because the dog took prizes. But that was nothing; if I were built like that I could take prizes myself. I wished I knew what kind of a dog it was, and what it was for, but I could not very well ask, for that would show that I did not know. Not that I want a dog like that, but only to know the secret of its birth.

I think he was going to hunt elephants with it, because I know, from remarks dropped by him, that he has hunted large game in India and Africa, and likes it. But I think that if he tries to hunt elephants with it, he is going to be disappointed. I do not believe that it is suited for elephants. It lacks energy, it lacks force of character, it lacks bitterness. These things all show in the meekness and resignation of its expression. It would not attack an elephant, I am sure of it. It might not run if it saw one coming, but it looked to me like a dog that would sit down and pray.

I wish he had told me what breed it was, if there are others; but I shall know the dog next time, and then if I can bring myself to it I will put delicacy aside and ask.

2 · WESTERN PORTRAITS

THE PONY EXPRESS

One of the most colorful but fleeting images that Mark Twain caught from the westward movement was the Pony Express rider. The Missouri traveler had the good fortune to make his stagecoach journey over the route followed by the Pony Express (St. Joseph, Missouri, to Sacramento, California) and during just that brief interval in American history (1860–61), before the completion of the telegraph line and the coming of the transcontinental railroad, when those swift horsemen were the only means of communication between the East and the

Far West. The sight of one of those riders, recorded in Roughing It *(1872), was one of the highlights of his trip west:*

In a little while all interest was taken up in stretching our
necks and watching for the "pony-rider"—the fleet messenger
who sped across the continent from St. Joe to Sacramento,
carrying letters nineteen hundred miles in eight days! Think
of that for perishable horse and human flesh and blood to do!
The pony-rider was usually a little bit of a man, brimful of
spirit and endurance. No matter what time of the day or night
his watch came on, and no matter whether it was winter or
summer, raining, snowing, hailing, or sleeting, or whether
his "beat" was a level straight road or a crazy trail over mountain crags and precipices, or whether it led through peaceful
regions or regions that swarmed with hostile Indians, he must
be always ready to leap into the saddle and be off like the
wind! There was no idling-time for a pony-rider on duty.
He rode fifty miles without stopping, by daylight, moonlight,
starlight, or through the blackness of darkness—just as it
happened. He rode a splendid horse that was born for a racer
and fed and lodged like a gentleman; kept him at his utmost
speed for ten miles, and then, as he came crashing up to the
station where stood two men holding fast a fresh, impatient
steed, the transfer of rider and mail-bag was made in the
twinkling of an eye, and away flew the eager pair and were
out of sight before the spectator could get hardly the ghost of
a look. Both rider and horse went "flying light." The rider's
dress was thin, and fitted close; he wore a "roundabout," and
a skull-cap, and tucked his pantaloons into his boot-tops like a
race-rider. He carried no arms—he carried nothing that was

not absolutely necessary, for even the postage on his literary freight was worth *five dollars a letter*. He got but little frivolous correspondence to carry—his bag had business letters in it, mostly. His horse was stripped of all unnecessary weight, too. He wore a little wafer of a racing-saddle, and no visible blanket. He wore light shoes, or none at all. The little flat mail-pockets strapped under the rider's thighs would each hold about the bulk of a child's primer. They held many and many an important business chapter and newspaper letter, but these were written on paper as airy and thin as gold-leaf, nearly, and thus bulk and weight were economized. The stage-coach traveled about a hundred to a hundred and twenty-five miles a day (twenty-four hours), the pony-rider about two hundred and fifty. There were about eighty pony-riders in the saddle all the time, night and day, stretching in a long, scattering procession from Missouri to California, forty flying eastward, and forty toward the west, and among them making four hundred gallant horses earn a stirring livelihood and see a deal of scenery every single day in the year.

We had had a consuming desire, from the beginning, to see a pony-rider, but somehow or other all that passed us and all that met us managed to streak by in the night, and so we heard only a whiz and a hail, and the swift phantom of the desert was gone before we could get our heads out of the windows. But now we were expecting one along every moment, and would see him in broad daylight. Presently the driver exclaims:

"HERE HE COMES!"

Every neck is stretched further, and every eye strained wider. Away across the endless dead level of the prairie a black speck appears against the sky, and it is plain that it moves. Well, I should think so! In a second or two it becomes a horse and rider, rising and falling, rising and falling—sweeping toward us nearer and nearer—growing more and more distinct, more and more sharply defined—nearer and still nearer, and the flutter of the hoofs comes faintly to the ear—another instant a whoop and a hurrah from our upper deck, a wave of the rider's hand, but no reply, and man and horse burst past our excited faces, and go swinging away like a belated fragment of a storm!

So sudden is it all, and so like a flash of unreal fancy, that but for the flake of white foam left quivering and perishing on a mail-sack after the vision had flashed by and disappeared, we might have doubted whether we had seen any actual horse and man at all, maybe.

THE TOWN-DOG AND THE COYOTE

All the sketches in this western section, except "Jim Baker's Blue Jay Yarn" and "The Celebrated Jumping Frog of Calaveras County," are in Mark Twain's Roughing It. *As the reader goes west in this book, he meets many strange creatures. One of those that fascinated Mark Twain the most was the coyote of the wild plains. In his description of this animal he introduces a dog that learns the truth about himself when he pursues his wild cousin:*

Along about an hour after breakfast we saw our first prairie-dog villages, the first antelope, and the first wolf. If I remember rightly, this latter was the regular *coyote* (pronounced ky-o-te) of the farther deserts. And if it was, he was not a pretty creature or respectable either, for I got well acquainted with his race afterward, and can speak with confidence. The coyote is a long, slim, sick-and-sorry-looking skeleton, with a grey wolf-skin stretched over it, a tolerably bushy tail that forever sags down with a despairing expression of forsakenness and misery, a furtive and evil eye, and a long sharp face, with slightly lifted lip and exposed teeth. He has a general slinking expression all over. The coyote is a living, breathing allegory of want. He is *always* hungry. He is always poor, out of luck, and friendless. The meanest creatures despise him, and even the fleas would desert him for a velocipede. He is so spiritless and cowardly that even while his exposed teeth are pretending a threat, the rest of his face is apologizing for it. And he is *so* homely!—so scrawny, and ribby, and coarse-haired, and pitiful. When he sees you he lifts his lip and lets a flash of his teeth out, and then turns a little out of the course he was pursuing, depresses his head a bit, and strikes a long, soft-footed trot through the sage-brush, glancing over his shoulder at you, from time to time, till he is about out of easy pistol range, and then he stops and takes a deliberate survey of you; he will trot fifty yards and stop again—another fifty and stop again; and finally the grey of his gliding body blends with the grey of the sage-brush, and he disappears. All this is when you make no demonstration against him; but if you do, he develops a livelier interest in his journey, and instantly electrifies his heels and puts such a deal of real estate between himself and your weapon that by the time you have raised the hammer you see that you need a minié rifle, and by the time you have got him in line you need a rifled cannon, and by the time you have "drawn a bead" on him you will see well enough that nothing but an unusually long-winded streak of lightning could reach him where he is now. But if you start a swift-footed dog after him, you will enjoy it ever so much—especially if it is a dog that has a good opinion of himself, and has been brought up to think he knows something about speed. The coyote will go swinging gently off on that deceitful trot of his, and every little while he will smile a fraudful smile over his shoulder that will fill that dog entirely full of encouragement and worldly ambition, and make him lay his head still lower to the ground, and stretch his neck farther to the front, and pant more fiercely, and stick his tail out straighter behind, and move his furious legs with a yet wilder frenzy, and leave a broader and broader, and higher and denser cloud of desert and smoking behind, and marking his long wake across the level plain! And all this time the dog is only a short twenty feet behind the coyote, and to save the soul of him he cannot understand why it is that he cannot get perceptibly closer; and he begins to get aggravated, and it makes him madder and madder to see how gently the coyote glides along and never pants or sweats or ceases to smile; and he grows still more and more incensed to see how shamefully he has been taken in by an entire stranger, and what an ignoble swindle that long, calm, softfooted trot is; and next he notices that he is getting fagged, and that the coyote actually has to slacken speed a little to keep from running away from him; and then that town-dog is mad in earnest, and he begins to strain and weep and swear, and paw the sand higher than ever, and reach for the coyote with concentrated and desperate energy. This "spurt" finds him six feet behind the gliding enemy, and two miles from his friends. And then, in the instant that a wild new hope is lighting up his face, the coyote turns and smiles blandly on him once more, and with something about it which seems to say: "Well, I shall have to tear myself away from you, bub: business is business, and it will not do for me to be fooling along this way all day"—and forthwith there is a rushing sound, and the sudden splitting of a long crack through the atmosphere, and behold that dog is solitary and alone in the midst of a vast solitude!

It makes his head swim. He stops, and looks all around, climbs the nearest sand-mound, and gazes into the distance; shakes his head reflectively; and then, without a word, he turns and jogs along back to his train, and takes up a humble position behind the hindmost waggon, and feels unspeakably mean, and looks ashamed, and hangs his tail at halfmast for a week. And for as much as a year after that, whenever there is a great hue and cry after a coyote, that dog will merely glance in that direction without emotion, and apparently observe to himself, "I believe I do not wish any of the pie."

HANK, THE BUFFALO-HUNTER

Horse—a "large, solid-hoofed, herbivorous mammal, domesticated by man since prehistoric times." If Mark Twain consulted the dictionary, he formed other ideas of this animal after he reached the buffalo country and the deserts of the American West. At least two horses he became acquainted with had never been domesticated enough to be either ridable or reliable. Fortunately for him, his first experience with western horses involved not himself but one of his traveling companions, who came off second best in a buffalo hunt:

Next morning just before dawn, when about five hundred and fifty miles from St. Joseph, our mud-wagon broke down. We were to be delayed five or six hours, and therefore we took horses, by invitation, and joined a party who were just starting on a buffalo hunt. It was noble sport galloping over the plain in the dewy freshness of the morning, but our part of the hunt ended in disaster and disgrace, for a wounded buffalo bull chased the passenger Bemis nearly two miles, and then he forsook his horse and took to a lone tree. He was very sullen about the matter for some twenty-four hours, but at last he began to soften little by little, and finally he said:

"Well, it was not funny, and there was no sense in those gawks making themselves so facetious over it. I tell you I was angry in earnest for awhile. I should have shot that long gangly lubber they called Hank, if I could have done it without crippling six or seven other people—but of course I couldn't, the old 'Allen' 's so confounded comprehensive. I wish those loafers had been up in the tree; they wouldn't have wanted to laugh so. If I had had a horse worth a cent—but no, the minute he saw that buffalo bull wheel on him and give a bellow, he raised straight up in the air and stood on his heels. The saddle began to slip, and I took him round the neck and laid close to him, and began to pray. Then he came down and stood up on the other end awhile, and the bull actually stopped pawing sand and bellowing to contemplate the inhuman spectacle. Then the bull made a pass at him and uttered a bellow that sounded perfectly frightful, it was so close to me, and that seemed to literally prostrate my horse's reason, and make a raving distracted maniac of him, and I wish I may die if he didn't stand on his head for a quarter of a minute and shed tears. He was absolutely out of his mind—he was, as sure as truth itself, and he really didn't know what he was doing. Then the bull came charging at us, and my horse dropped down on all fours and took a fresh start—and then for the next ten minutes he would actually throw one handspring after another so fast that the bull began to get unsettled, too, and didn't know where to start in—and so he stood there sneezing, and shoveling dust over his back, and bellowing every now and then, and thinking he had got a fifteen-hundred dollar circus horse for breakfast, certain. Well, I was first out on his neck—the horse's, not the bull's—and then underneath, and next on his rump, and sometimes head up, and sometimes heels—but I tell you it seemed solemn and awful to be ripping and tearing and carrying on so in the presence of death, as you might say. Pretty soon the bull made a snatch for us and brought away some of my horse's tail (I suppose, but do not know, being pretty busy at the time), but *something* made him hungry for solitude and suggested to him to get up and hunt for it. And then you ought to have seen that spider-legged old skeleton go! and you ought to have seen the bull cut out after him, too—head down, tongue out, tail up, bellow-ing like everything, and actually mowing down the weeds, and tearing up the earth, and boosting up the sand like a whirlwind! By George, it was a hot race! I and the saddle were back on the rump, and I had the bridle in my teeth and holding on to the pommel with both hands. First we left the dogs behind; then we passed a jackass rabbit; then we over-took a coyote, and were gaining on an antelope when the rot-ten girths let go and threw me about thirty yards off to the left, and as the saddle went down over the horse's rump he gave it a lift with his heels that sent it more than four hundred yards up in the air, I wish I may die in a minute if he didn't. I fell at the foot of the only solitary tree there was in nine counties adjacent (as any creature could see with the naked eye), and the next second I had hold of the bark with four sets of nails and my teeth, and the next second after that I was astraddle of the main limb and blaspheming my luck in a way that made my breath smell of brimstone. I *had* the bull, now, if he did not think of *one* thing. But that one thing I dreaded. I dreaded it very seriously. There was a possibility that the bull might not think of it, but there were greater chances that he would. I made up my mind what I would do in case he did. It was a little over forty feet to the ground from where I sat. I cautiously unwound the lariat from the pommel of my saddle—"

"Your *saddle?* Did you take your saddle up in the tree with you?"

"Take it up in the tree with me? Why, how you talk. Of course I didn't. No man could do that. It *fell* in the tree when it came down."

"Oh—exactly."

"Certainly. I unwound the lariat, and fastened one end of it to the limb. It was the very best green raw-hide, and capable of sustaining tons. I made a slip-noose in the other end, and then hung it down to see the length. It reached down twenty-two feet—half way to the ground. I then loaded every barrel of the Allen with a double charge. I felt satisfied. I said to myself, if he never thinks of that one thing that I dread, all right—but if he does, all right anyhow—I am fixed for him.

But don't you know that the very thing a man dreads is the thing that always happens? Indeed it is so. I watched the bull, now, with anxiety—anxiety which no one can conceive of who has not been in such a situation and felt that at any moment death might come. Presently a thought came into the bull's eye. I knew it! said I—if my nerve fails now, I am lost. Sure enough, it was just as I had dreaded, he started in to climb the tree—"

"What, the bull?"

"Of course—who else?"

"But a bull can't climb a tree."

"He can't, can't he? Since you know so much about it, did you ever see a bull try?"

"No! I never dreamt of such a thing."

"Well, then, what is the use of your talking that way, then? Because you never saw a thing done, is that any reason why it can't be done?"

"Well, all right—go on. What did you do?"

"The bull started up, and got along well for about ten feet, then slipped and slid back. I breathed easier. He tried it again —got up a little higher—slipped again. But he came at it once more, and this time he was careful. He got gradually higher and higher, and my spirits went down more and more. Up he came—an inch at a time—with his eyes hot, and his tongue hanging out. Higher and higher—hitched his foot over the stump of a limb, and looked up, as much as to say, 'You are my meat, friend.' Up again—higher and higher, and getting more excited the closer he got. He was within ten feet of me! I took a long breath,—and then said I, 'It is now or never.' I had the coil of the lariat all ready; I paid it out slowly, till it hung right over his head; all of a sudden I let go of the slack, and the slipnoose fell fairly round his neck! Quicker than lightning I out with the Allen and let him have it in the face. It was an awful roar, and must have scared the bull out of his senses. When the smoke cleared away, there he was, dangling in the air, twenty foot from the ground, and going out of one convulsion into another faster than you could count! I didn't stop to count, anyhow—I shinned down the tree and shot for home."

"Bemis, is all that true, just as you have stated it?"

"I wish I may rot in my tracks and die the death of a dog if it isn't."

"Well, we can't refuse to believe it, and we don't. But if there were some proofs—"

"Proofs! Did I bring back my lariat?"

"No."

"Did I bring back my horse?"

"No."

"Did you ever see the bull again?"

"No."

"Well, then, what more do you want? I never saw anybody as particular as you are about a little thing like that."

I made up my mind that if this man was not a liar he only missed it by the skin of his teeth.

TOM QUARTZ, THE DYNAMITE CAT

In the following episode, Mark Twain writes in a different vein, using the anecdotal and dialectal method of "The Celebrated Jumping Frog of Calaveras County" and "Jim Baker's Blue-Jay Yarn." The reader will also recognize in the cari-

*catured portrait a foretaste of the animated cartoon art of
Walt Disney and a whole school of modern animal fablers.*

One of my comrades there—another of those victims of
eighteen years of unrequited toil and blighted hopes—was
one of the gentlest spirits that ever bore its patient cross in a
weary exile: grave and simple Dick Baker, pocket-miner of
Dead-Horse Gulch.—He was forty-six, gray as a rat, earnest,
thoughtful, slenderly educated, slouchily dressed and clay-
soiled, but his heart was finer metal than any gold his shovel
ever brought to light—than any, indeed, that ever was mined
or minted.

Whenever he was out of luck and a little down-hearted, he
would fall to mourning over the loss of a wonderful cat he
used to own (for where women and children are not, men of
kindly impulses take up with pets, for they must love something). And he always spoke of the strange sagacity of that cat
with the air of a man who believed in his secret heart that
there was something human about it—may be even supernatural.

I heard him talking about this animal once. He said:

"Gentlemen, I used to have a cat here, by the name of Tom
Quartz, which you'd a took an interest in I reckon—most any
body would. I had him here eight year—and he was the re-
markablest cat *I* ever see. He was a large gray one of the Tom
specie, an' he had more hard, natchral sense than any man in
this camp—'n' a *power* of dignity—he wouldn't let the
Gov'ner of Californy be familiar with him. He never ketched
a rat in his life—'peared to be above it. He never cared for
nothing but mining. He knowed more about mining, that

cat did, than any man *I* ever, ever see. You couldn't tell *him* noth'n' 'bout placer diggin's—'n' as for pocket mining, why he was just born for it. He would dig out after me an' Jim when we went over the hills prospect'n', and he would trot along behind us for as much as five mile, if we went so fur. An' he had the best judgment about mining ground—why you never see anything like it. When we went to work, he'd scatter a glance around, 'n' if he didn't think much of the indications, he would give a look as much as to say, "Well, I'll have to get you to excuse *me*," 'n' without another word he'd hyste his nose into the air 'n' shove for home. But if the ground suited him, he would lay low 'n' keep dark till the first pan was washed, 'n' then he would sidle up 'n' take a look, an' if there was about six or seven grains of gold *he* was satisfied—he didn't want no better prospect 'n' that—'n' then he would lay down on our coats and snore like a steamboat till we'd struck the pocket, an' then get up 'n' superintend. He was nearly lightin' on superintending.

"Well, by an' by, up comes this yer quartz excitement. Every body was into it—every body was pick'n' 'n' blast'n' instead of shovelin' dirt on the hill side—every body was put'n' down a shaft instead of scrapin' the surface. Noth'n would do Jim, but *we* must tackle the ledges, too, 'n' so we did. We commence put'n down a shaft, 'n' Tom Quartz he begin to wonder what in the Dickens it was all about. *He* hadn't ever seen any mining like that before, 'n' he was all upset, as you may say—he couldn't come to a right understanding of it no way—it was too many for *him*. He was down on it, too, you bet you—he was down on it powerful—'n' always appeared to consider it the cussedest foolishness out. But that cat, you know, was *always* agin new fangled arrangements—some-how he never could abide 'em. *You* know how it is with old habits. But by an' by Tom Quartz begin to git sort of recon-ciled a little, though he never *could* altogether understand that eternal sinkin' of a shaft an' never pannin' out any thing. At last he got to comin' down in the shaft, hisself, to try to cipher it out. An' when he'd git the blues, 'n' feel kind of scruffy, 'n' aggravated 'n' disgusted—knowin' as he did, that the bills was runnin' up all the time an' we warn't makin' a cent—he would curl up on a gunny sack in the corner an' go to sleep. Well, one day when the shaft was down about eight foot, the rock got so hard that we had to put in a blast—the first blast'n' we'd ever done since Tom Quartz was born. An' then we lit the fuse 'n' clumb out 'n' gott off 'bout fifty yards—'n' forgot 'n' left Tom Quartz sound asleep on the gunny sack. In 'bout a minute we seen a puff of smoke bust up out of the hole, 'n' then everything let go with an awful crash, 'n' about four million tons of rocks 'n' dirt 'n' smoke 'n' splinters shot up 'bout a mile an' a half into the air, an' by George, right in the dead centre of it was old Tom Quartz a goin' end over end, an' a snortin' an' a sneez'n', an' a clawin' an' a reachin' for things like all possessed. But it warn't no use, you know, it warn't no use. An' that was the last we see of *him* for about two minutes 'n' a half, an' then all of a sudden it begin to rain rocks and rubbage, an' directly he come down ker-whop about ten foot off f'm where we stood. Well, I reckon he was p'raps the orneriest lookin' beast you ever see. One ear was sot back on his neck, 'n' his tail was stove up, 'n' his eye-winkers was swinged off, 'n' he was all blacked up with powder an' smoke, an' all sloppy with mud 'n' slush f'm one end to the other.

Well sir, it warn't no use to try to apologize—we couldn't say a word. He took a sort of a disgusted look at hisself, 'n' then he looked at us—an' it was just exactly the same as if he had said—'Gents, may be *you* think it's smart to take advantage of a cat that ain't had no experience of quartz minin', but *I* think *different*'—an' then he turned on his heel 'n' marched off home without ever saying another word.

"That was jest his style. An' may be you won't believe it, but after that you never see a cat so prejudiced agin' quartz mining as what he was. An' by an' by when he *did* get to goin' down in the shaft agin, you'd a been astonished at his sagacity. The minute we'd tetch off a blast 'n' the fuse'd begin to sizzle, he'd give a look as much as to say: 'Well, I'll have to git you to excuse *me*,' an' it was surpris'n' the way he'd shin out of that hole 'n' go f'r a tree. Sagacity? It ain't no name for it. 'Twas *inspiration*!"

I said, "Well, Mr. Baker, his prejudice against quartz-mining *was* remarkable, considering how he came by it. Couldn't you ever cure him of it?"

"*Cure him*! No! When Tom Quartz was sot once, he was *always* sot—and you might a blowed him up as much as three million times 'n' you'd never a broken him of his cussed prejudice agin quartz mining."

The affection and the pride that lit up Baker's face when he delivered this tribute to the firmness of his humble friend of other days, will always be a vivid memory with me.

JIM BAKER'S BLUE-JAY YARN

Mark Twain learned a great deal about wild creatures and prided himself on some rather intimate insights into their be-

havior, especially that of birds. But the man who understood birds better than Mark Twain himself was an old-timer in the California mountains by the name of Jim Baker. At least Jim claimed *that he understood birds, even their very language, as Mark Twain recounts in his* A Tramp Abroad *(1880):*

Animals talk to each other, of course. There can be no question about that; but I suppose there are very few people who can understand them. I never knew but one man who could. I knew he could, however, because he told me so himself. He was a middle-aged, simple-hearted miner who had lived in a lonely corner of California, among the woods, and mountains, a good many years, and had studied the ways of his only neighbors, the beasts and the birds, until he believed he could accurately translate any remark which they made. This was *Jim Baker.* According to Jim Baker, some animals have only a limited education, and use only very simple words, and scarcely ever a comparison or a flowery figure; whereas, certain other animals have a large vocabulary, a fine command of language and a ready and fluent delivery; consequently these latter talk a great deal; they like it; they are conscious of their talent, and they enjoy "showing off." Baker said, that after long and careful observation, he had come to the conclusion that the blue-jays were the best talkers he had found among birds and beasts. Said he:

"There's more *to* a blue-jay than any other creature. He has got more moods, and more different kinds of feelings than other creatures; and, mind you, whatever a blue-jay feels, he can put into language. And no mere commonplace language, either, but rattling, out-and-out book-talk—and bristling with

34

metaphor, too—just bristling! And as for command of language—why *you* never see a blue-jay get stuck for a word. No
man ever did. They just boil out of him! And another thing:
I've noticed a good deal, and there's no bird, or cow, or anything that uses as good grammar as a blue-jay. You may say
a cat uses good grammar. Well, a cat does—but you let a cat
get excited once; you let a cat get to pulling fur with another
cat on a shed, nights, and you'll hear grammar that will give
you lockjaw. Ignorant people think it's the *noise* which fight-
ing cats make that is so aggravating, but it ain't so; it's the
sickening grammar they use. Now I've never heard a jay use
bad grammar but very seldom; and when they do, they are as
ashamed as a human; they shut right down and leave.

"You may call a jay a bird. Well, so he is, in a measure—
because he's got feathers on him, and don't belong to no
church, perhaps; but otherwise he is just as much a human as
you be. And I'll tell you for why. A jay's gifts, and instincts,
and feelings, and interests, cover the whole ground. A jay
hasn't got any more principle than a Congressman. A jay will
lie, a jay will steal, a jay will deceive, a jay will betray; and four
times out of five, a jay will go back on his solemnest promise.
The sacredness of an obligation is a thing which you can't
cram into no blue-jay's head. Now, on top of all this, there's
another thing; a jay can out-swear any gentleman in the mines.
You think a cat can swear. Well, a cat can; but you give a
blue-jay a subject that calls for his reserve powers, and where
is your cat? Don't talk to *me*—I know too much about this
thing. And there's yet another thing; in the one little particular of scolding—just good, clean, out-and-out scolding—a
blue-jay can lay over anything, human or divine. Yes, sir, a

35

jay is everything that a man is. A jay can cry, a jay can laugh, a jay can feel shame, a jay can reason and plan and discuss, a jay likes gossip and scandal, a jay has got a sense of humor, a jay knows when he is an ass just as well as you do—maybe better. If a jay ain't human, he better take in his sign, that's all. Now I'm going to tell you a perfectly true fact about some blue-jays."

"When I first begun to understand jay language correctly, there was a little incident happened here. Seven years ago, the last man in this region but me moved away. There stands his house,—been empty ever since; a log house, with a plank roof —just one big room, and no more; no ceiling—nothing between the rafters and the floor. Well, one Sunday morning I was sitting out here in front of my cabin, with my cat, taking the sun, and looking at the blue hills, and listening to the leaves rustling so lonely in the trees, and thinking of the home away yonder in the States, that I hadn't heard from in thirteen years, when a blue-jay lit on that house, with an acorn in his mouth, and says, 'Hello, I reckon I've struck something.' When he spoke, the acorn dropped out of his mouth and rolled down the roof, of course, but he didn't care; his mind was all on the thing he had struck. It was a knot-hole in the roof. He cocked his head to one side, shut one eye and put the other one to the hole, like a 'possum looking down a jug; then he glanced up with his bright eyes, gave a wink or two with his wings—which signifies gratification, you understand,— and says, 'It looks like a hole, it's located like a hole,—blamed if I don't believe it *is* a hole!'

"Then he cocked his head down and took another look; he glances up perfectly joyful, this time; winks his wings and his tail both, and says, 'O, no, this ain't no fat thing, I reckon! If I ain't in luck!—why it's a perfectly elegant hole!' So he flew down and got that acorn, and fetched it up and dropped it in, and was just tilting his head back, with the heavenliest smile on his face, when all of a sudden he was paralyzed into a listening attitude and that smile faded gradually out of his countenance like breath off'n a razor, and the queerest look of surprise took its place. Then he says, 'Why, I didn't hear it fall!' He cocked his eye at the hole again, and took a long look; raised up and shook his head; stepped around to the other side of the hole and took another look from that side; shook his head again. He studied a while, then he just went into the *details*—walked round and round the hole and spied into it from every point of the compass. No use. Now he took a thinking attitude on the comb of the roof and scratched the back of his head with his right foot a minute, and finally says, 'Well, it's too many for *me*, that's certain; must be a mighty long hole; however, I ain't got no time to fool around here, I got to 'tend to business; I reckon it's all right—chance it, anyway.'

"So he flew off and fetched another acorn and dropped it in, and tried to flirt his eye to the hole quick enough to see what become of it, but he was too late. He held his eye there as much as a minute; then he raised up and sighed, and says, 'Confound it, I don't seem to understand this thing, no way; however, I'll tackle her again.' He fetched another acorn, and done his level best to see what become of it, but he couldn't. He says, 'Well, *I* never struck no such a hole as this before; I'm of the opinion it's a totally new kind of a hole.' Then he begun to get mad. He held in for a spell, walking up and down the comb

of the roof and shaking his head and muttering to himself; but
his feelings got the upper hand of him, presently, and he
broke loose and cussed himself black in the face. I never see a
bird take on so about a little thing. When he got through he
walks to the hole and looks in again for half a minute; then he
says, 'Well, you're a long hole, and a deep hole, and a mighty
singular hole altogether—but I've started in to fill you, and
I'm d——d if I *don't* fill you, if it takes a hundred years!'

"And with that, away he went. You never see a bird work
so since you was born. He laid into his work like a nigger, and
the way he hove acorns into that hole for about two hours and
a half was one of the most exciting and astonishing spectacles
I ever struck. He never stopped to take a look any more—he
just hove 'em in and went for more. Well, at last he could
hardly flop his wings, he was so tuckered out. He comes a-
drooping down, once more, sweating like an ice-pitcher, drops
his acorn in and says, '*Now* I guess I've got the bulge on you
by this time!' So he bent down for a look. If you'll believe me,
when his head come up again he was just pale with rage. He
says, 'I've shoveled acorns enough in there to keep the family
thirty years, and if I can see a sign of one of 'em I wish I may
land in a museum with a belly full of sawdust in two minutes!'

"He just had strength enough to crawl up on to the comb
and lean his back agin the chimbly, and then he collected his
impressions and begun to free his mind. I see in a second that
what I had mistook for profanity in the mines was only just
the rudiments, as you may say.

"Another jay was going by, and heard him doing his devo-
tions, and stops to inquire what was up. The sufferer told him
the whole circumstance, and says, 'Now yonder's the hole,

38

and if you don't believe me, go and look for yourself.' So this fellow went and looked, and comes back and says, 'How many did you say you put in there?' 'Not any less than two tons,' says the sufferer. The other jay went and looked again. He couldn't seem to make it out, so he raised a yell, and three more jays come. They all examined the hole, they all made the sufferer tell it over again, then they all discussed it, and got off as many leather-headed opinions about it as an average crowd of humans could have done.

"They called in more jays; then more and more, till pretty soon this whole region 'peared to have a blue flush about it. There must have been five thousand of them; and such another jawing and disputing and ripping and cussing, you never heard. Every jay in the whole lot put his eye to the hole and delivered a more chuckle-headed opinion about the mystery than the jay that went there before him. They examined the house all over, too. The door was standing half open, and at last one old jay happened to go and light on it and look in. Of course that knocked the mystery galley-west in a second. There lay the acorns, scattered all over the floor. He flopped his wings and raised a whoop. 'Come here!' he says, 'Come here, everybody; hang'd if this fool hasn't been trying to fill up a house with acorns!' They all came a-swooping down like a blue cloud, and as each fellow lit on the door and took a glance, the whole absurdity of the contract that that first jay had tackled hit him home and he fell over backwards suffocating with laughter, and the next jay took his place and done the same.

"Well, sir, they roosted around here on the house-top and the trees for an hour, and guffawed over that thing like human beings. It ain't any use to tell me a blue-jay hasn't got a sense of humor, because I know better. And memory, too. They brought jays here from all over the United States to look down that hole, every summer for three years. Other birds too. And they could all see the point, except an owl that come from Nova Scotia to visit the Yo Semite, and he took this thing in on his way back. He said he couldn't see anything funny in it. But then he was a good deal disappointed about Yo Semite, too."

A GENUINE MEXICAN PLUG

Realizing what a greenhorn he was on his first arrival in Nevada, Mark Twain was determined to become a real Westerner in as short a time as possible. But his ambition was greater than his knowledge of horseflesh or his talent for riding. In Roughing It *he relates an encounter in* Virginia City *with a broncho that left him with a livid posterior and a vivid memory for years to come:*

I resolved to have a horse to ride. I had never seen such wild, free, magnificent horsemanship outside of a circus as these picturesquely clad Mexicans, Californians, and Mexicanized Americans displayed in Carson streets every day. How they rode! Leaning just gently forward out of the perpendicular, easy and nonchalant, with broad slouch-hat brim blown square up in front, and long *riata* swinging above the head, they swept through the town like the wind! The next minute they were only a sailing puff of dust on the far desert. If they trotted, they sat up gallantly and gracefully, and seemed part of the horse; did not go jiggering up and down after the silly Miss-Nancy fashion of the riding-schools. I had quickly learned to tell a horse from a cow, and was full of anxiety to learn more. I was resolved to buy a horse.

While the thought was rankling in my mind, the auctioneer came scurrying through the plaza on a black beast that had as many humps and corners on him as a dromedary, and was necessarily uncomely; but he was "going, going, at twenty-two!—horse, saddle and bridle at twenty-two dollars, gentlemen!" and I could hardly resist.

A man whom I did not know (he turned out to be the auctioneer's brother) noticed the wistful look in my eye, and observed that that was a very remarkable horse to be going at such a price; and added that the saddle alone was worth the money. It was a Spanish saddle, with ponderous *tapidaros*, and furnished with the ungainly sole-leather covering with the unspellable name. I said I had half a notion to bid. Then this keen-eyed person appeared to me to be "taking my measure"; but I dismissed the suspicion when he spoke, for his manner was full of guileless candor and truthfulness. Said he:

"I know that horse—know him well. You are a stranger, I take it, and so you think he was an American horse, maybe, but I assure you he is not. He is nothing of the kind; but— excuse my speaking in a low voice, other people being near— he is, without the shadow of a doubt, a Genuine Mexican Plug!"

I did not know what a Genuine Mexican Plug was, but there was something about this man's way of saying it, that made me swear inwardly that I would own a Genuine Mexican Plug, or die.

"Has he any other—er—advantages?" I inquired, suppressing what eagerness I could.

He hooked his forefinger in the pocket of my army shirt, led me to one side, and breathed in my ear impressively these words:

"He can out-buck anything in America!"

"Going, going, going—at *twent-ty*-four dollars and a half, gen—" "Twenty-seven!" I shouted, in a frenzy.

"And sold!" said the auctioneer, and passed over the Genuine Mexican Plug to me.

I could scarcely contain my exultation. I paid the money, and put the animal in a neighboring livery stable to dine and rest himself.

In the afternoon I brought the creature into the plaza, and certain citizens held him by the head, and others by the tail, while I mounted him. As soon as they let go, he placed all his feet in a bunch together, lowered his back, and then suddenly arched it upward, and shot me straight into the air a matter of three or four feet! I came as straight down again, lit in the saddle, went instantly up again, came down almost on the pommel, shot up again, and came down on the horse's neck— all in the space of three or four seconds. Then he rose and stood almost straight up on his hind feet, and I, clasping his lean neck desperately, slid back onto the saddle, and held on. He came down, and immediately hoisted his heels into the air, delivering a vicious kick at the sky, and stood on his fore feet. And then down he came once more, and began the original exercise of shooting me straight up again.

The third time I went up I heard a stranger say: "Oh, *don't* he buck, though!"

While I was up, somebody struck the horse a sounding thwack with a leathern strap, and when I arrived again the

Genuine Mexican Plug was not there. A Californian youth chased him up and caught him, and asked if he might have a ride. I granted him that luxury. He mounted the Genuine, got lifted into the air once, but sent his spurs home as he descended, and the horse darted away like a telegram. He soared over three fences like a bird, and disappeared down the road toward the Washoe Valley.

I sat down on a stone with a sigh, and by a natural impulse one of my hands sought my forehead, and the other the base of my stomach. I believe I never appreciated, till then, the poverty of the human machinery—for I still needed a hand or two to place elsewhere. Pen cannot describe how I was jolted up. Imagination cannot conceive how disjointed I was—how internally, externally, and universally I was unsettled, mixed up, and ruptured. There was a sympathetic crowd around me, though.

One elderly-looking comforter said:

"Stranger, you've been taken in. Everybody in this camp knows that horse. Any child, any Injun, could have told you that he'd buck; he is the very worst devil to buck on the continent of America. You hear *me*. I'm Curry. Old *Abe* Curry. And moreover, he is a simon-pure, out-and-out, genuine d——d Mexican plug, and an uncommon mean one at that, too. Why, you turnip, if you had laid low and kept dark, there's chances to buy an *American* horse for mighty little more than you paid for that bloody old foreign relic."

I gave no sign; but I made up my mind that if the auctioneer's brother's funeral took place while I was in the territory I would postpone all other recreations and attend it.

After a gallop of sixteen miles the Californian youth and

the Genuine Mexican Plug came tearing into town again, shedding foam-flakes like the spume-spray that drives before a typhoon, and, with one final skip over a wheelbarrow and a Chinaman, cast anchor in front of the "ranch."

Such panting and blowing! Such spreading and contracting of the red equine nostrils, and glaring of the wild equine eye! But was the imperial beast subjugated? Indeed, he was not. His lordship the Speaker of the House thought he was, and mounted him to go down to the Capitol; but the first dash the creature made was over a pile of telegraph-poles half as high as a church; and his time to the Capitol—one mile and three-quarters—remains unbeaten to this day. But then he took an advantage—he left out the mile, and only did the three-quarters. That is to say, he made a straight cut across lots, preferring fences and ditches to a crooked road; and when the Speaker got to the Capitol he said he had been in the air so much he felt as if he had made the trip on a comet.

In the evening the Speaker came home afoot for exercise, and got the Genuine towed back behind a quartz-wagon. The next day I loaned the animal to the Clerk of the House to go down to the Dana silver-mine, six miles, and *he* walked back for exercise, and got the horse towed. Everybody I loaned him to always walked back; they never could get enough exercise any other way. Still, I continued to loan him to anybody who was willing to borrow him, my idea being to get him crippled, and throw him on the borrower's hands, or killed, and make the borrower pay for him. But somehow nothing ever happened to him. He took chances that no other horse ever took and survived, but he always came out safe. It was his daily habit to try experiments that had always before been con-

44

sidered impossible, but he always got through. Sometimes he miscalculated a little, and did not get his rider through intact, but *he* always got through himself. Of course I had tried to sell him; but that was a stretch of simplicity which met with little sympathy. The auctioneer stormed up and down the streets on him for four days, dispersing the populace, interrupting business, and destroying children, and never got a bid—at least never any but the eighteen-dollar one he hired a notoriously substanceless bummer to make. The people only smiled pleasantly, and restrained their desire to buy, if they had any. Then the auctioneer brought in his bill, and I withdrew the horse from the market. We tried to trade him off at private vendue next, offering him at a sacrifice for second-hand tombstones, old iron, temperance tracts—any kind of property. But holders were stiff, and we returned from the market again. I never tried to ride the horse any more. Walking was good enough exercise for a man like me, that had nothing the matter with him except ruptures, internal injuries, and such things. Finally I tried to *give* him away. But it was a failure. Parties said earthquakes were handy enough on the Pacific coast—they did not wish to own one. As a last resort I offered him to the Governor for the use of the "Brigade." His face lit up eagerly at first, but toned down again, and he said the thing would be too palpable.

Just then the livery-stable man brought in his bill for six weeks' keeping—stall-room for the horse, fifteen dollars; hay for the horse, two hundred and fifty! The Genuine Mexican Plug had eaten a ton of the article, and the man said he would have eaten a hundred if he had let him.

I will remark here, in all seriousness, that the regular price of hay during that year and a part of the next was really two hundred and fifty dollars a ton. During a part of the previous year it had sold at five hundred a ton, in gold, and during the winter before that there was such a scarcity of the article that in several instances small quantities had brought eight hundred dollars a ton in coin! The consequence might be guessed without my telling it: people turned their stock loose to starve, and before the spring arrived Carson and Eagle Valleys were almost literally carpeted with their carcasses! Any old settler there will verify these statements.

I managed to pay the livery bill, and that same day I gave the Genuine Mexican Plug to a passing Arkansas emigrant whom fortune delivered into my hand. If this ever meets his eye, he will doubtless remember the donation.

Now whoever has had the luck to ride a real Mexican plug will recognize the animal depicted in this chapter, and hardly consider him exaggerated—but the uninitiated will feel justified in regarding his portrait as a fancy sketch, perhaps.

THE JACKASS RABBIT

Blue-jays were insolent, coyotes were crafty skulkers, buffaloes were lords of the domain, and western horses looked out for themselves. But the western jack rabbit, Mark Twain discovered, was an inoffensive little animal that survived on an admirable mixture of curiosity, panic, and speed:

As the sun was going down, we saw the first specimen of an animal familiarly known over two thousand miles of mountain and desert—from Kansas clear to the Pacific Ocean—as the "jackass rabbit." He is well named. He is just like any other

46

rabbit, except that he is from one-third to twice as large, has longer legs in proportion to his size, and has the most preposterous ears that ever were mounted on any creature *but* a jackass. When he is sitting quiet, thinking about his sins, or is absent-minded or unapprehensive of danger, his majestic ears project above him conspicuously; but the breaking of a twig will scare him nearly to death, and then he tilts his ears back gently and starts for home. All you can see, then, for the next minute, is his long gray form stretched out straight and "streaking it" through the low sage-brush, head erect, eyes right, and ears just canted a little to the rear, but showing you where the animal is, all the time, the same as if he carried a jib. Now and then he makes a marvelous spring with his long legs, high over the stunted sage-brush, and scores a leap that would make a horse envious. Presently, he comes down to a long, graceful "lope," and shortly he mysteriously disappears. He has crouched behind a sage-brush, and will sit there and listen and tremble until you get within six feet of him, when he will get under way again. But one must shoot at this creature once, if he wishes to see him throw his heart into his heels, and do the best he knows how. He is frightened clear through, now, and he lays his long ears down on his back, straightens himself out like a yard-stick every spring he makes, and scatters miles behind him with an easy indifference that is enchanting.

Our party made this specimen "hump himself," as the conductor said. The Secretary started him with a shot from the Colt; I commenced spitting at him with my weapon; and all in the same instant the old Allen's whole broadside let go with a rattling crash, and it is not putting it too strong to say that the rabbit was frantic! He dropped his ears, set up his tail, and left for San Francisco at a speed which can only be described as a flash and a vanish! Long after he was out of sight we could hear him whiz.

THE CELEBRATED JUMPING FROG OF CALAVERAS COUNTY

The story that first made Mark Twain a nationally—even internationally—famous humorist is a sketch he wrote about three western characters: Simon Wheeler, an old-timer of the early California mining-camps; Jim Smiley, a vagabond gambler; and a stranger. "The Celebrated Jumping Frog of Calaveras County" is really a double story, an anecdote within a tale. While he relates his anecdote within the framework of Mark Twain's story, Simon Wheeler reveals himself as one of the most interesting characters of our Western tradition: he is an endless talker, an ungrammatical fellow but with a gift of colorful language, a treasure-house of local folklore, and a master at making fascinating tales out of both commonplace and impossible materials. Jim Smiley, the hero of Wheeler's tale, is another part of our Western tradition: a deceitful fellow with a weakness for gambling, who is outwitted by a stranger more shrewd than himself. Along with these Westerners, Mark Twain weaves into his story three characters from his animal world: a racing nag, an undefeatable bulldog, and an educated jumping frog. Each of these characters, human and animal, becomes a portrait in itself, and the story that Mark Twain develops around all six turns out to be one of the classics of American literature.

In compliance with the request of a friend of mine, who wrote

me from the East, I called on good-natured, garrulous old
Simon Wheeler, and inquired after my friend's friend,
Leonidas W. Smiley, as requested to do, and I hereunto append
the result. I have a lurking suspicion that *Leonidas W.* Smiley
is a myth; that my friend never knew such a personage; and
that he only conjectured that if I asked old Wheeler about it,
it would remind him of his infamous *Jim* Smiley, and he
would go to work and bore me to death with some exasperat-
ing reminiscence of him as long and as tedious as it should be
useless to me. If that was the design, it succeeded.

I found Simon Wheeler dozing comfortably by the bar-
room stove of the dilapidated tavern in the decayed mining
camp of Angel's, and I noticed that he was fat and bald-
headed, and had an expression of winning gentleness and
simplicity upon his tranquil countenance. He roused up, and
gave me good day. I told him that a friend of mine had commissioned me to make some inquiries about a cherished companion of his boyhood named *Leonidas W.* Smiley—*Rev.
Leonidas W.* Smiley, a young minister of the Gospel, who he
had heard was at one time a resident of Angel's Camp. I added
that if Mr. Wheeler could tell me anything about this Rev.
Leonidas W. Smiley, I would feel under many obligations
to him.

Simon Wheeler backed me into a corner and blockaded
me there with his chair, and then sat down and reeled off the
monotonous narrative which follows this paragraph. He
never smiled, he never frowned, he never changed his voice
from the gentle-flowing key to which he tuned his initial
sentence, he never betrayed the slightest suspicion of enthusiasm; but all through the interminable narrative there ran

a vein of impressive earnestness and sincerity, which showed
me plainly that, so far from his imagining that there was anything ridiculous or funny about his story, he regarded it as a
really important matter, and admired its two heroes as men
of transcendent genius in *finesse*. I let him go on in his own
way, and never interrupted him once.

"Rev. Leonidas W. H'm, Reverend Le—well, there was a
feller once by the name of *Jim* Smiley, in the winter of '49—
or maybe it was the spring of '50—I don't recollect exactly,
somehow, though what makes me think it was one or the
other is because I remember the big flume warn't finished
when he first come to the camp; but anyway, he was the
curiousest man about always betting on anything that turned
up you ever see, if he could get anybody to bet on the other
side; and if he couldn't he'd change sides. Any way that suited
the other man would suit *him*—any way just so's he got a bet,
he was satisfied. But still he was lucky, uncommon lucky; he
most always come out winner. He was always ready and laying for a chance; there couldn't be no solit'ry thing mentioned
but that feller'd offer to bet on it, and take any side you please,
as I was just telling you. If there was a horse-race, you'd find
him flush or you'd find him busted at the end of it; if there
was a dog-fight, he'd bet on it; if there was a cat-fight, he'd
bet on it; if there was a chicken-fight, he'd bet on it; why, if
there was two birds setting on a fence, he would bet you which
one would fly first; or if there was a camp-meeting, he would
be there reg'lar to bet on Parson Walker, which he judged to
be the best exhorter about here, and so he was too, and a good
man. If he even see a straddlebug start to go anywheres, he
would bet you how long it would take him to get to—to

wherever he was going to, and if you took him up, he would foller that straddlebug to Mexico but what he would find out where he was bound for and how long he was on the road. Lots of the boys here has seen that Smiley, and can tell you about him. Why, it never made no difference to him—he'd bet on any thing—the dangdest feller. Parson Walker's wife laid very sick once, for a good while, and it seemed as if they warn't going to save her; but one morning he come in, and Smiley up and asked him how she was, and he said she was considerable better—thank the Lord for his inf'nite mercy—and coming on so smart that with the blessing of Prov'dence she'd get well yet; and Smiley, before he thought, says, 'Well, I'll resk two-and-a-half she don't anyway.'

"Thish-yer Smiley had a mare—the boys called her the fifteen-minute nag, but that was only in fun, you know, because of course she was faster than that—and he used to win money on that horse, for all she was so slow and always had the asthma, or the distemper, or the consumption, or something of that kind. They used to give her two or three hundred yards' start, and then pass her under way; but always at the fag end of the race she'd get excited and desperate like, and come cavorting and straddling up, and scattering her legs around limber, sometimes in the air, and sometimes out to one side among the fences, and kicking up m-o-r-e dust and raising m-o-r-e racket with her coughing and sneezing and blowing her nose—and *always* fetch up at the stand just about a neck ahead, as near as you could cipher it down.

"And he had a little small bull-pup, that to look at him you'd think he warn't worth a cent but to set around and look ornery and lay for a chance to steal something. But as soon as money was up on him he was a different dog; his under-jaw'd begin to stick out like the fo'castle of a steamboat, and his teeth would uncover and shine like the furnaces. And a dog might tackle him and bully-rag him, and bite him, and throw him over his shoulder two or three times, and Andrew Jackson—which was the name of the pup—Andrew Jackson would never let on but what *he* was satisfied, and hadn't expected nothing else—and the bets being doubled and doubled on the other side all the time, till the money was all up; and then all of a sudden he would grab that other dog jest by the j'int of his hind leg and freeze to it—not chaw, you understand, but only just grip and hang on till they throwed up the sponge, if it was a year. Smiley always come out winner on that pup, till he harnessed a dog once that didn't have no hind legs, because they'd been sawed off in a circular saw, and when the thing had gone along far enough, and the money was all up, and he come to make a snatch for his pet holt, he see in a minute how he'd been imposed on, and how the other dog had him in the door, so to speak, and he 'peared surprised, and then he looked sorter discouraged-like, and he didn't try no more to win the fight, and so he got shucked out bad. He give Smiley a look, as much as to say his heart was broke, and it was *his* fault, for putting up a dog that hadn't no hind legs for him to take holt of, which was his main dependence in a fight, and then he limped off a piece and laid down and died. It was a good pup, was that Andrew Jackson, and would have made a name for hisself if he'd lived, for the stuff was in him and he had genius—I know it, because he hadn't no opportunities to speak of, and it don't stand to reason that a dog could make such a fight as he could under them circumstances if he hadn't no talent. It always makes me feel sorry when I think of that last fight of his'n, and the way it turned out.

"Well, thish-yer Smiley had rat-tarriers, and chicken cocks, and tomcats and all them kind of things, till you couldn't rest, and you couldn't fetch nothing for him to bet on but he'd match you. He ketched a frog one day, and took him home, and said he cal'lated to educate him; and so he never done nothing for three months but set in his back yard and learn that frog to jump. And you bet he *did* learn him, too. He'd give him a little punch behind, and the next minute you'd see that frog whirling in the air like a doughnut—see him turn one summerset, or maybe a couple, if he got a good start, and come down flat-footed and all right, like a cat. He got him up so in the matter of ketching flies, and kep' him in practice so constant, that he'd nail a fly every time as fur as he could see him. Smiley said all a frog wanted was education, and he could do 'most anything—and I believe him. Why, I've seen him set Dan'l Webster down here on this floor—Dan'l Webster was the name of the frog—and sing out, 'Flies, Dan'l, flies!' and quicker'n you could wink he'd spring straight up and snake a fly off'n the counter there, and flop down on the floor ag'in as solid as a gob of mud, and fall to scratching the side of his head with his hind foot as indifferent as if he hadn't no idea he'd been doin' any more'n any frog might do. You never see a frog so modest and straightfar'ard as he was, for all he was so gifted. And when it come to fair and square jumping on a dead level, he could get over more ground at one straddle than any animal of his breed you ever see. Jumping on a dead level was his strong suit, you understand; and when it come to that, Smiley would ante up money on him as long as he had a red.

Smiley was monstrous proud of his frog, and well he might be, for fellers that had traveled and been everywheres all said he laid over any frog that ever *they* see.

"Well, Smiley kep' the beast in a little lattice box, and he used to fetch him downtown sometimes and lay for a bet. One day a feller—a stranger in the camp, he was—come acrost him with his box, and says:

" 'What might it be that you've got in the box?'

"And Smiley says, sorter indifferent-like, 'It might be a parrot, or it might be a canary, maybe, but it ain't—it's only just a frog.'

"And the feller took it, and looked at it careful, and turned it round this way and that, and says, 'H'm—so 'tis. Well, what's *he* good for?'

" 'Well,' Smiley says, easy and careless, 'he's good enough for *one* thing, I should judge—he can outjump any frog in Calaveras County.'

"The feller took the box again, and took another long, particular look, and give it back to Smiley, and says, very deliberate, 'Well,' he says, 'I don't see no p'ints about that frog that's any better'n any other frog.'

" 'Maybe you don't,' Smiley says. 'Maybe you understand frogs and maybe you don't understand 'em; maybe you've had experience, and maybe you ain't only a amature, as it were. Anyways, I've got *my* opinion, and I'll resk forty dollars that he can outjump any frog in Calaveras County.'

"And the feller studied a minute, and then says, kinder sad-like, 'Well, I'm only a stranger here, and I ain't got no frog; but if I had a frog, I'd bet you.'

"And then Smiley says, 'That's all right—that's all right—

if you'll hold my box a minute, I'll go and get you a frog.' And so the feller took the box, and put up his forty dollars along with Smiley's, and set down to wait.

"So he set there a good while thinking and thinking to himself, and then he got the frog out and prized his mouth open and took a teaspoon and filled him full of quail-shot—filled him pretty near up to his chin—and set him on the floor. Smiley he went to the swamp and slopped around in the mud for a long time, and finally he ketched a frog, and fetched him in, and give him to this feller, and says:

" 'Now, if you're ready, set him alongside of Dan'l, with his fore paws just even with Dan'l's, and I'll give the word.' Then he says, 'One—two—three—git!' and him and the feller touched up the frogs from behind, and the new frog hopped off lively, but Dan'l give a heave, and hysted up his shoulders —so—like a Frenchman, but it warn't no use—he couldn't budge; he was planted as solid as a church, and he couldn't no more stir than if he was anchored out. Smiley was a good deal surprised, and he was disgusted too, but he didn't have no idea what the matter was, of course.

"The feller took the money and started away; and when he was going out at the door, he sorter jerked his thumb over his shoulder—so—at Dan'l, and says again, very deliberate, 'Well,' he says, '*I* don't see no p'ints about that frog that's any better'n any other frog.'

"Smiley he stood scratching his head and looking down at Dan'l a long time, and at last he says, 'I do wonder what in the nation that frog throw'd off for—I wonder if there ain't something the matter with him—he 'pears to look mighty baggy, somehow.' And he ketched Dan'l by the nap of the neck, and

55

hefted him, and says, 'Why blame my cats if he don't weigh five pound!' and turned him upside down and he belched out a double handful of shot. And then he see how it was, and he was the maddest man—he set the frog down and took out after that feller, but he never ketched him. And—"

[Here Simon Wheeler heard his name called from the front yard, and got up to see what was wanted.] And turning to me as he moved away, he said: "Just set where you are, stranger, and rest easy—I ain't going to be gone a second."

But, by your leave, I did not think that a continuation of the history of the enterprising vagabond *Jim* Smiley would be likely to afford me much information concerning the Rev. *Leonidas W.* Smiley, and so I started away.

At the door I met the sociable Wheeler returning, and he buttonholed me and recommenced:

"Well, thish-yer Smiley had a yaller one-eyed cow that didn't have no tail, only just a short stump like a bannanner, and—"

However, lacking both time and inclination, I did not wait to hear about the afflicted cow, but took my leave.

3 · EXOTICS

When Mark Twain and his fellow travelers went ashore at the French seaport of Marseilles during a voyage through the Mediterranean, he and a friend were attracted to one of the oddest collections of animals he had ever seen. In The Innocents Abroad *(1869), he describes the following:*

In the great Zoological Gardens we found specimens of all the animals the world produces, I think, including a dromedary, a monkey ornamented with tufts of brilliant blue and carmine

57

hair—a very gorgeous monkey he was—a hippopotamus from the Nile, and a sort of tall, long-legged bird with a beak like a powder-horn, and close-fitting wings like the tails of a dress-coat. This fellow stood up with his eyes shut and his shoulders stooped forward a little, and looked as if he had his hands under his coat-tails. Such tranquil stupidity, such supernatural gravity, such self-righteousness, and such ineffable self-complacency as were in the countenance and attitude of that gray-bodied, dark-winged, bald-headed, and preposterously uncomely bird! He was so ungainly, so pimply about the head, so scaly about the legs; yet so serene, so unspeakably satisfied! He was the most comical-looking creature that can be imagined. It was good to hear Dan and the doctor laugh—such natural and such enjoyable laughter had not been heard among our excursionists since our ship sailed away from America. This bird was a godsend to us, and I should be an ingrate if I forgot to make honorable mention of him in these pages. Ours was a pleasure excursion; therefore we stayed with that bird an hour, and made the most of him. We stirred him up occasionally, but he only unclosed an eye and slowly closed it again, abating no jot of his stately piety of demeanor or his tremendous seriousness. He only seemed to say, "Defile not Heaven's anointed with unsanctified hands." We did not know his name, and so we called him "The Pilgrim." Dan said:

"All he wants now is a Plymouth Collection."

The boon companion of the colossal elephant was a common cat! This cat had a fashion of climbing up the elephant's hind legs, and roosting on his back. She would sit up there, with her paws curved under her breast, and sleep in the sun half the afternoon. It used to annoy the elephant at first, and he would reach up and take her down, but she would go aft and climb up again. She persisted until she finally conquered the elephant's prejudices, and now they are inseparable friends. The cat plays about her comrade's fore feet or his trunk often, until dogs approach, and then she goes aloft out of danger. The elephant has annihilated several dogs lately, that pressed his companion too closely.

THE INSULTING RAVEN

More than any other creatures of the animal kingdom, birds reminded Mark Twain of human beings. In his many encounters with birds at home and abroad, he found repeatedly that they were the greatest mimickers and gossips of the animal world. He recorded their amusing antics in many sketches in his travel books, such as the following from A Tramp Abroad:

One afternoon I got lost in the woods about a mile from the hotel, and presently fell into a train of dreamy thought about animals which talk. . . . I finally got to imagining I glimpsed small flitting shapes here and there down the columned aisles of the forest. . . . It was a pine wood, with so thick and soft a carpet of brown needles that one's footfall made no more sound than if he were treading on wool; the tree-trunks were as round and straight and smooth as pillars. . . . The world was bright with sunshine outside, but a deep and mellow twilight reigned in there, and also a silence so profound that I seemed to hear my own breathings. A raven suddenly uttered a hoarse croak over my head. It made me start; and then I was angry because I started. I looked up, and the creature was sitting on a limb right over me, looking down at me. . . . I eyed the raven, and the raven eyed me. Nothing was said during some seconds. Then the bird stepped a little way along his limb to get a better point of observation, lifted his wings, stuck his head far down below his shoulders toward me, and croaked again—a croak with a distinctly insulting expression about it. If he had spoken in English he could not have said any more plainly than he did say in raven, "Well, what do *you* want here?" I felt as foolish as if I had been caught in some mean act. . . . However, I made no reply; I would not bandy words with a raven. The adversary waited a while, with his shoulders still lifted, his head thrust down between them, and his keen bright eye fixed on me; then he threw out two or three more insults, which I could not understand, further than that I knew a portion of them consisted of language not used in church.

I still made no reply. Now the adversary raised his head and called. There was an answering croak from a little distance in the wood—evidently a croak of inquiry. The adversary explained with enthusiasm, and the other raven dropped everything and came. The two sat side by side on the limb and discussed me as freely and offensively as two great naturalists might discuss a new kind of bug. The thing became more and more embarrassing. They called in another friend. This was too much. I saw that they had the advantage of me, and so I concluded to get out of the scrape by walking out of it. They enjoyed my defeat as much as any low white people could have done. They craned their necks and laughed at me (for a raven *can* laugh, just like a man), they squalled insulting remarks after me as long as they could see me. They were nothing but ravens—I knew that—what they thought about me could be a matter of no consequence—and yet when even a raven shouts after you, "What a hat! Oh, pull down your vest!" and that sort of thing, it hurts you and humiliates you, and there is no getting around it with fine reasoning and pretty arguments.

A NATURALIST TAVERN

In this same Black Forest region of Germany, Mark Twain and his traveling companion stopped overnight at the unique "Naturalist Tavern," where they enjoyed the oddest collection of domesticated wild animals. This passage and "The Aimless Ant" which follows are also from A Tramp Abroad.

In the morning we took breakfast in the garden, under the trees, in the delightful German summer fashion. The air was filled with the fragrance of flowers and wild animals. . . . There were great cages populous with fluttering and chattering foreign birds and other great cages and greater wire pens, populous with quadrupeds, both native and foreign. There were some free creatures, too, and quite sociable ones they were. White rabbits went loping about the place, and occasionally came and sniffed at our shoes and shins; a fawn, with a red ribbon on its neck, walked up and examined us fearlessly; rare breeds of chickens and doves begged for crumbs, and a poor tailless raven hopped about with a humble, shame-faced mien which said, "Please do not notice my exposure,—think how you would feel in my circumstances, and be charitable." If he was observed too much, he would retire behind something and stay there until he judged the party's interest had found another object. I never have seen another dumb creature that was so morbidly sensitive.

THE AIMLESS ANT

Mark Twain was skeptical about many popular ideas concerning the animal world. Curiosity and a compulsion to get at the truth of such matters often led him to study even the most insignificant creatures for hours at a time. One day he sat down in the Black Forest to observe the behavior of the common ant, just to settle his doubts about this "industrious" little fellow:

Now and then, while we rested, we watched the laborious ant at his work. I found nothing new in him—certainly nothing to change my opinion of him. It seems to me that in the matter of intellect the ant must be a strangely overrated bird. During many summers, now, I have watched him, when I ought to have been in better business, and I have not yet come across a living ant that seemed to have any more sense than a dead one. I refer to the ordinary ant, of course; I have had no experience of those wonderful Swiss and African ones which vote, keep drilled armies, hold slaves, and dispute about religion. Those particular ants may be all that the naturalist paints them, but I am persuaded that the average ant is a sham. I admit his industry, of course; he is the hardest-working creature in the world—when anybody is looking—but his leather-headedness is the point I make against him. He goes out foraging, he makes a capture, and then what does he do? Go home? No—he goes anywhere but home. He doesn't know where home is. His home may be only three feet away—no matter, he can't find it. He makes his capture, as I have said; it is generally something which can be of no sort of use to himself or anybody else; it is usually seven times bigger than it ought to be; he hunts out the awkwardest place to take hold of it; he lifts it bodily up in the air by main force, and starts; not toward home, but in the opposite direction; not calmly and wisely, but with a frantic haste which is wasteful of his strength; he fetches up against a pebble, and instead of going around it, he climbs over it backward dragging his booty after him, tumbles down on the other side, jumps up in a passion, kicks the dust off his clothes, moistens his hands, grabs his property viciously, yanks it this way, then that, shoves it ahead of him a moment, turns tail and lugs it after him another moment, gets madder and madder, then presently hoists it into the air and goes tearing away in an entirely new direction; comes to a weed; it never occurs to him to go around it; no, he must climb it; and he does climb it, dragging his worthless property to the top—which is as bright a thing to do as is would be for me to carry a sack of flour from Heidelberg to Paris by way of Strasburg steeple; when he gets up there he finds that that is not the place; takes a cursory glance at the scenery and either climbs down again or tumbles down, and starts off once more—as usual, in a new direction. At the end of half an hour, he fetches up within six inches of the place he started from and lays his burden down; meantime he has been over all the ground for two yards around, and climbed all the weeds and pebbles he came across. Now he wipes the sweat from his brow, strokes his limbs, and then marches aimlessly off, in as violent a hurry as ever. He traverses a good deal of zigzag country, and by and by stumbles on his same booty again. He does not remember to have ever seen it before; he looks around to see which is not the way home, grabs his bundle and starts; he goes through the same adventures he had before; finally stops to rest, and a friend comes along. Evidently the friend remarks that a last year's grasshopper's leg is a very noble acquisition, and inquires where he got it. Evidently the proprietor does not remember exactly where he did get it, but thinks he got it "around here somewhere." Evidently the friend contracts to help him freight it home. Then, with a judgment peculiarly antic (pun not intentional), they take hold of opposite ends of that grasshopper leg and begin to tug with all their might in opposite directions. Presently they take a rest and confer together. They decide that something is wrong, they can't make out what. Then they go at it again, just as before. Same result. Mutual recriminations follow. Evidently each accuses the other of being an obstructionist. They warm up, and the dispute ends in a fight. They lock themselves together and chew each other's jaws for a while; then they roll and tumble on the ground till one loses a horn or a leg and has to haul off for repairs. They make up and go to work again in the same old insane way, but the crippled ant is at a disadvantage; tug as he may, the other one drags off the booty and him at the end of it. Instead of giving up, he hangs on, and gets his shins bruised against every obstruction that comes in the way. By and by, when that grasshopper leg has been dragged all over the same old ground once more, it is finally dumped at about the spot where it originally lay, the two perspiring ants inspect it thoughtfully and decide that dried grasshopper legs are a poor sort of property after all, and then each starts off in a different direction to see if he can't find an old nail or something else that is heavy enough to afford entertainment and at the same time valueless enough to make an ant want to own it. . . .

Science has recently discovered that the ant does not lay up anything for winter use. This will knock him out of literature, to some extent. He does not work, except when people are looking, and only then when the observer has a green, naturalistic look, and seems to be taking notes.

"JERICHO," THE MOST SPIRITED HORSE ON EARTH

While caravaning through the Holy Land, Mark Twain was equally bemused by his Lebanese horse, whose odd behavior he set down in The Innocents Abroad.

While I am speaking of animals, I will mention that I have a horse now by the name of "Jericho." He is a mare. I have seen remarkable horses before, but none so remarkable as this. I wanted a horse that could shy, and this one fills the bill. I had an idea that shying indicated spirit. If I was correct, I have got the most spirited horse on earth. He shies at everything he comes across, with the utmost impartiality. He appears to have a mortal dread of telegraph-poles, especially; and it is fortunate that these are on both sides of the road, because as it is now, I never fall off twice in succession on the same side. If I fell on the same side always, it would get to be monotonous after a while. This creature has scared at everything he has seen today, except a haystack. He walked up to that with intrepidity and a recklessness that were astonishing. And it

65

would fill any one with admiration to see how he preserves his self-possession in the presence of a barley sack. This dare devil bravery will be the death of this horse some day.

He is not particularly fast, but I think he will get me through the Holy Land. He has only one fault. His tail has been chopped off or else he has sat down on it too hard, some time or other, and he has to fight the flies with his heels. This is all very well, but when he tries to kick a fly off the top of his head with his hind foot, it is too much variety. He is going to get himself into trouble that way some day. He reaches around and bites my legs, too. I do not care particularly about that, only I do not like to see a horse too sociable.

I think the owner of this prize had a wrong opinion about him. He had an idea that he was one of those fiery, untamed steeds, but he is not of that character. I know the Arab had this idea, because when he brought the horse out for inspection in Beirout, he kept jerking at the bridle and shouting in Arabic, "Whoa! will you? Do you want to run away, you ferocious beast, and break your neck?" when all the time the horse was not doing anything in the world, and only looked like he wanted to lean up against something and think. Whenever he is not shying at things, or reaching after a fly, he wants to do that yet. How it would surprise his owner to know this.

THE SYRIAN CAMEL

During this same journey the Western humorist recorded his impressions of a true Middle East exotic, the Syrian camel:

The road was filled with mule-trains and long processions of camels. This reminds me that we have been trying for some time to think what a camel looks like, and now we have made it out. When he is down on all his knees, flat on his breast to receive his load, he looks something like a goose swimming; and when he is upright he looks like an ostrich with an extra set of legs. Camels are not beautiful, and their long under-lip gives them an exceedingly "gallus" expression. They have immense flat, forked cushions of feet, that make a track in the dust like a pie with a slice cut out of it. They are not particular about their diet. They would eat a tombstone if they could bite it. A thistle grows about here which has needles on it that would pierce through leather, I think; if one touches you, you can find relief in nothing but profanity. The camels eat these. They show by their actions that they enjoy them. I suppose it would be a real treat to a camel to have a keg of nails for supper.

THE SYRIAN CAMEL'S APPETITE

Several years later, in Roughing It, *Mark Twain observed that only the western jackass and mule would eat the tough sagebrush of the American deserts. As an afterthought, he expanded the image with similar hyperbole to the statement that these creatures "will eat pine-knots, or anthracite coal, or brass filings, or lead pipe, or old bottles, or anything that comes handy, and then go off looking as grateful as if they had had oysters for dinner." As if playing upon a now well-established theme, Twain recalled the camels described above and developed the theme into a full-bodied portrait and anecdote:*

Mules and donkeys and camels have appetites that anything will relieve temporarily, but nothing satisfy. In Syria, once, at the headwaters of the Jordan, a camel took charge of my overcoat while the tents were being pitched, and examined it with a critical eye, all over, with as much interest as if he had an idea of getting one made like it; and then, after he was done figuring on it as an article of apparel, he began to contemplate it as an article of diet. He put his foot on it, and lifted one of the sleeves out with his teeth, and chewed and chewed at it, gradually taking it in, and all the while opening and closing his eyes in a kind of religious ecstasy, as if he had never tasted anything as good as an overcoat before in his life. Then he smacked his lips once or twice, and reached after the other sleeve. Next he tried the velvet collar, and smiled a smile of such contentment that it was plain to see that he regarded that as the daintiest thing about an overcoat. The tails went next, along with some percussion-caps and cough-candy, and some fig-paste from Constantinople. And then my newspaper correspondence dropped out, and he took a chance in that—manuscript letters written for the home papers. But he was treading on dangerous ground, now. He began to come across solid wisdom in those documents that was rather weighty on his stomach; and occasionally he would take a joke that would shake him up till it loosened his teeth; it was getting to be perilous times with him, but he held his grip with good courage and hopefully, till at last he began to stumble on statements that not even a camel would swallow with impunity. He began to gag and gasp, and his eyes to stand out, and his forelegs to spread, and in about a quarter of a minute he fell over as stiff as a carpenter's work-bench, and died a death of indescribable agony. I went and pulled the manuscript out of his mouth, and found that the sensitive creature

68

had choked to death on one of the mildest and gentlest state-ments of fact that I ever laid before a trusting public.

The anecdote is preposterous, of course, but the portrait itself is saved from becoming just another piece of gross exaggera-tion by Mark Twain's straight-faced, matter-of-fact beginning, his precise description of a camel's behavior, and his dash of satire on professional humorists and journalism. The reader, who throughout life is offered printed fare equally indigest-ible, can hardly reject the idea of a camel smiling, then gag-ging on the "statements of fact" of professional journalists. Moreover, the reader will have no difficulty accepting this story if he has already accepted talking blue-jays and buffaloes climbing trees. Mark Twain's generation and our own have been long conditioned to the portrayal of animals as human beings by a tradition as old as Aesop and as new as Walt Disney.

AUSTRALIAN ODDITIES

On his lecture tour around the world in 1895–96, Mark Twain seems to have been almost as much interested in the animal inhabitants of the Far East as he was in the people of that region. The "fauna of Australasia" furnished much material for his Following the Equator. *As his boat neared Sydney and the "island wilderness" of Australia, he recorded many vignettes of sea creatures: "large schools of whales in the dis-tance" compared with which "nothing could be daintier than the puffs of vapor they spout when seen against the pink glory of the sinking sun, or against the dark mass of an island reposing in the deep blue shadow of a storm cloud." Or "flocks of flying fish—slim, shapely, graceful, and intensely white.*

With the sun on them they look like a flight of silver fruit-knives. They are able to fly a hundred yards." He notes that Sydney Harbor was "populous with the finest breeds of man-eating sharks in the world." Out of the lore about these sharks Mark Twain spun an apochryphal story about Cecil Rhodes (see page 84).

During interludes of sight-seeing on his lecture tour of the land "down under," the American humorist found time to record his impressions of many exotic birds of the region. The most beautiful, he found, were the bird of paradise and the lyre bird. But those that held a special fascination for him were the oddities, especially the extinct Great Moa, which a naturalist told him "stood thirteen feet high, and could step over an ordinary man's head or kick his hat off; and his head, too, for that matter. He said it was wingless, but a swift runner. The natives used to ride it. It could make forty miles an hour, and keep it up for four hundred miles and come out reasonably fresh. It was still in existence when the railway was introduced into New Zealand; still in existence and carrying the mails." His informant also told Mark Twain about a less exaggerated Australian bird called the bell-bird, "the creature that at short intervals all day rings out its mellow and exquisite peal from the deeps of the forest. It is the favorite and best friend of the weary and thirsty sundowner tramp; for he knows that wherever the bell-bird is, there is water." On his way to visit an agricultural college in Australia, Mark Twain noted that "we saw the usual birds—the beautiful little green parrots, the magpie . . . and also the slender bird of modest plumage and eternally forgettable name—the bird that is the smartest among birds, and can give a parrot 30 to 1 in the game and then talk him to death." Twain's impressions of the magpie are particularly reminiscent of his early portraits of California blue-jays and Black Forest ravens:

The magpie was out in great force, in the fields and on the fences. He is a handsome large creature, with snowy white decorations, and is a singer; he has a murmurous rich note that is lovely. He was once modest, even diffident; but he lost all that when he found out that he was Australia's sole musical bird. He has talent, and cuteness, and impudence; and in his tame state he is a most satisfactory pet—never coming when he is called, always coming when he isn't, and studying disobedience as an accomplishment. He is not confined, but loafs all over the house and grounds, like the laughing jackass. I think he learns to talk, I know he learns to sing tunes, and his friends say that he knows how to steal without learning. I was acquainted with a tame magpie in Melbourne. He had lived in a lady's house several years, and believed he owned it. The lady had tamed him, and in return he had tamed the lady. He was always on deck when not wanted, always having his own way, always tyrannizing over the dog, and always making the cat's life a slow sorrow and a martyrdom. He knew a number of tunes and could sing them in perfect time and tune; and would do it, too, at any time that silence was wanted; and then encore himself and do it again; but if he was asked to sing he would go out and take a walk.

The strangest Australasian quadruped in Mark Twain's Following the Equator, *described to the American by an English naturalist, was the ornithorhyncus, more commonly known as the duck-bill. "Nature's fondness for dabbling in the erratic*

71

*was most notably exhibited in that curious combination of
bird, fish, amphibian, burrower, crawler, and quadruped . . .
grotesquest of animals, king of the animalculae of the world
for versatility of character and make-up." Mark Twain took
pains to record precisely his naturalist friend's description:*

You can call it anything you want to, and be right. It is a fish,
for it lives in the river half the time; it is an amphibian, since
it likes both and does not know which it prefers; it is a hiber-
nian, for when times are dull and nothing much going on it
buries itself under the mud at the bottom of a puddle and
hibernates there a couple of weeks at a time; it is a kind of
duck, for it has a duck-bill and four webbed paddles; it is a
fish and quadruped together, for in the water it swims with
the paddles and on shore it paws itself across country with
them; it is a kind of seal, for it has a seal's fur; it is carnivorous,
herbivorous, insectivorous, and vermifuginous, for it eats fish
and grass and butterflies, and in the season digs worms out of
the mud and devours them; it is clearly a bird, for it lays eggs
and hatches them; it is clearly a mammal, for it nurses its
young.

*Mark Twain learned, and dutifully reported, that the kanga-
roo, most famous of the marsupials, was a freakish survival of
an archaic world, like the ornithorhyncus. The naturalist had
written verses about both of these creatures:*

> *Come forth from thy oozy couch,*
>   *Ornithorhyncus dear!*
> *And greet with a cordial claw*
>   *The stranger that longs to hear*

From thy own lips the tale
Of thy origin all unknown:
Thy misplaced bone where flesh should be
And flesh where should be bone;

And fishy fin where should be paw,
And beaver-trowel tail,
And snout of beast equip'd with teeth
Where gills ought to prevail.

Come, Kangeroo, the good and true!
Foreshortened as to legs,
And body tapered like a churn,
And sack marsupial, i fegs,

And tell us why you linger here,
Though relic of a vanquished time,
When all your friends as fossils sleep,
Immortalized in lime!

Fascinated by the very idea of the preposterous duck-bill, Mark Twain developed a temporary obsession over this creature's scientific name. During the rest of his tour of Australasia, although he was even less a poet than the naturalist, he repeatedly challenged himself to write similar verses in which he could concoct words rhyming with ornithorhyncus. *This preoccupation became a standing joke among his lecture audiences.*

THE DINGO

Mark Twain always had what the American humor authority Walter Blair calls "a greedy curiosity" about animals. Birds and horses most often excited his interest, probably because

73

of the human attributes he detected in them; but dogs of special distinction would elicit an observation. In Australia it was a wild dog called the "dingo":

He was a beautiful creature—shapely, graceful and a little wolfish in some of his aspects, but with a most friendly eye and sociable disposition. The dingo is not an importation; he was present in great force when the whites first came to the continent. It may be said that he is the oldest dog in the universe; his origin, his descent, the places where his ancestors first appeared, are as unknown and as untraceable as the camel's. He is the most precious dog in the world because he does not bark. But in an evil hour he got to raiding the sheepruns to appease his hunger, and that sealed his doom. He is hunted now just as if he were a wolf.

ELEPHANTS

Several months and thousands of miles later, Mark Twain was marveling at the flora and fauna of India. On his lecture tour through the subcontinent, he recorded in Following the Equator *many brief but graphic impressions of exotic creatures he had not seen elsewhere. The predatory creatures of the jungle, such as tigers and snakes, were only staggering statistics to him; but the confusion of human beings and domestic animals caught his eye at every turn of the journey, which, he wrote, "was full of interest both night and day, for the country road was never quiet, never empty, but was always India in motion, always a streaming flood of brown people clothed in smouchings from the rainbow, a tossing and moiling flood, happy, noisy, a charming and satisfying confusion*

of strange human and strange animal life and equally strange
and outlandish vehicles." The animals he saw in a typical inn
yard had the air of being at home there much as the animals
on a farm home did in early days of America:

By the veranda stood a palm, and a monkey lived in it, and led
a lonesome life, and always looked sad and weary, and the
crows bothered him a good deal.

The inn cow poked about the compound and emphasized
the secluded and country air of the place, and there was a dog
of no particular breed, who was always present in the compound, and always asleep, always stretched out baking in the
sun and adding to the deep tranquillity and reposefulness of
the place, when the crows were away on business. White-
draperied servants were coming and going all the time, but
they seemed only spirits, for their feet were bare and made
no sound. Down the lane a piece lived an elephant in the
shade of a noble tree, and rocked and rocked, and reached
about with his trunk, begging of his brown mistress or fumb-
ling the children playing at his feet. And there were camels
about, but they go on velvet feet, and were proper to the silence
and serenity of the surroundings.

Of all this medley, the elephants most fascinated Mark Twain.
In the midst of a description of the teeming life and cramped
quarters of an Indian city, he wrote:

Imagine a file of elephants marching through such a crevice
of a street and scraping the paint off both sides of it with their
hides. How big they must look, and how little they must make

75

the houses look; and when the elephants are in their glittering court costume, what a contrast they must make with the humble and sordid surroundings. And when a mad elephant goes raging through, belting right and left with his trunk, how do these swarms of people get out of the way? I suppose it is a thing which happens now and then in the mad season (for elephants have a mad season). . . .

By and by to the elephant stables, and I took a ride; but it was by request—I did not ask for it, and didn't want it; but I took it, because otherwise they would have thought I was afraid, which I was. The elephant kneels down, by command —one end of him at a time—and you climb the ladder and get into the howdah, and then he gets up, one end at a time, just as a ship gets up over a wave; and after that, as he strides monstrously about, his motion is much like a ship's motion. The mahout bores into the back of his head with a great iron prod, and you wonder at his temerity and at the elephant's patience, and you think that perhaps the patience will not last; but it does, and nothing happens. The mahout talks to the elephant in a low voice all the time, and the elephant seems to understand it all and to be pleased with it; and he obeys every order in the most contented and docile way. Among these twenty-five elephants were two which were larger than any I had ever seen before, and if I had thought I could learn to not be afraid, I would have taken one of them while the police were not looking.

Mark Twain could not resist another opportunity to ride one of these creatures and enjoy a few moments of superiority over his fellow human beings:

We wandered contentedly around here and there in India; to Lahore, among other places, where the Lieutenant-Governor lent me an elephant. This hospitality stands out in my experiences in a stately isolation. It was a fine elephant, affable, gentlemanly, educated, and I was not afraid of it. I even rode it with confidence through the crowded lanes of the native city, where it scared all the horses out of their senses, and where children were always just escaping its feet. It took the middle of the road in a fine, independent way, and left it to the world to get out of the way or take the consequences. I am used to being afraid of collisions when I ride or drive, but when one is on top of an elephant that feeling is absent. I could have ridden in comfort through a regiment of runaway teams. I could easily learn to prefer an elephant to any other vehicle, partly because of that immunity from collisions, and partly because of the fine view one has from up there, and partly because of the dignity one feels in that high place, and partly because one can look in at the windows and see what is going on privately among the family. The Lahore horses were used to elephants, but they were rapturously afraid of them just the same. It seemed curious. Perhaps the better they know the elephant the more they respect him in that peculiar way. In our own case we are not afraid of dynamite till we get acquainted with it.

THE MONKEYS OF DELHI

Even in historic Delhi Mark Twain's attention was diverted by the behavior of animals. Here it was the monkeys that inhabited the grounds of a famous old mansion:

77

It stands in a great garden—oriental fashion—and about it are many noble trees. The trees harbor monkeys; and they are monkeys of a watchful and enterprising sort, and not much troubled with fear. They invade the house whenever they get a chance, and carry off everything they don't want. One morning the master of the house was in his bath, and the window was open. Near it stood a pot of yellow paint and a brush. Some monkeys appeared in the window; to scare them away, the gentleman threw his sponge at them. They did not scare at all; they jumped into the room and threw yellow paint all over him from the brush, and drove him out; then they painted the walls and the floor and the tank and the windows and the furniture yellow, and were in the dressing-room painting that when help arrived and routed them.

Two of these creatures came into my room in the early morning, through a window whose shutters I had left open, and when I woke one of them was before the glass brushing his hair, and the other one had my note-book, and was reading a page of humorous notes and crying. I did not mind the one with the hair-brush, but the conduct of the other one hurt me; it hurts me yet. I threw something at him, and that was wrong, for my host had told me that the monkeys were best left alone. They threw everything at me that they could lift, and then went into the bathroom to get some more things, and I shut the door on them.

THE ROWDY CROWS OF INDIA

If Mark Twain could not tolerate offensive monkeys, he could feel indulgent toward even the most raucous birds. Unlike the more exotic creatures of the Far East, birds were a nostalgic

reminder of home and early years, and their human-like be-
havior gave the humorist more scope for character portrayal.
"Jim Baker's Blue-Jay Yarn," spun out of Mark Twain's
California days, and his portrait of the Black Forest, done
during his first trip into Germany, are climaxed seventeen
years later by his sketch of another species that invaded his
privacy in Bombay:

Some natives—I don't remember how many—went into my
bedroom, now, and put things to rights and arranged the
mosquito-bar, and I went to bed to nurse my cough. It was
about nine in the evening. What a state of things! For three
hours the yelling and shouting of natives in the hall continued,
along with the velvety patter of their swift bare feet—what a
racket it was! They were yelling orders and messages down
three flights. Why, in the matter of noise it amounted to a
riot, an insurrection, a revolution. And then there were other
noises mixed up with these and at intervals tremendously ac-
centing them—roofs falling in, I judged, windows smashing,
persons being murdered, crows squawking, and deriding, and
cursing, canaries screeching, monkeys jabbering, macaws blaspheming, and every now and then fiendish bursts of laughter
and explosions of dynamite. By midnight I had suffered all the
different kinds of shocks there are, and knew that I could
never more be disturbed by them, either isolated or in combination. Then came peace—stillness deep and solemn—and
lasted till five.

Then it all broke loose again. And who restarted it? The
Bird of Birds—the Indian crow. I came to know him well, by
and by, and be infatuated with him. I suppose he is the hardest

lot that wears feathers. Yes, and the cheerfulest, and the best satisfied with himself. He never arrived at what he is by any careless process, or any sudden one; he is a work of art, and "art is long"; he is the product of immemorial ages, and of deep calculation; one can't make a bird like that in a day. He has been reincarnated more times than Shiva; and he has kept a sample of each incarnation, and fused it into his constitution. In the course of his evolutionary promotions, his sublime march toward ultimate perfection, he has been a gambler, a low comedian, a dissolute priest, a fussy woman, a blackguard, a scoffer, a liar, a thief, a spy, an informer, a trading politician, a swindler, a professional hypocrite, a patriot for cash, a reformer, a lecturer, a lawyer, a conspirator, a rebel, a royalist, a democrat, a practicer and propagator of irreverence, a meddler, an intruder, and a wallower in sin for the mere love of it. The strange result, the incredible result, of this patient accumulation of all damnable traits is, that he does not know what care is, he does not know what sorrow is, he does not know what remorse is; his life is one long thundering ecstasy of happiness, and he will go to his death untroubled, knowing that he will soon turn up again as an author or something, and be even more intolerably capable and comfortable than ever he was before.

In his straddling wide forward-step, and his springy sidewise series of hops, and his impudent air, and his cunning way of canting his head to one side upon occasion, he reminds one of the American blackbird. But the sharp resemblances stop there. He is much bigger than the blackbird; and he lacks the blackbird's trim and slender and beautiful build and shapely beak; and of course his sober garb of gray and rusty black is a poor and humble thing compared with the splendid luster of the blackbird's metallic sables and shifting and flashing bronze glories. The blackbird is a perfect gentleman, in deportment and attire, and is not noisy, I believe, except when holding religious services and political conventions in a tree; but this Indian sham Quaker is just a rowdy, and is always noisy when awake—always chaffing, scolding, scoffing, laughing, ripping, and cursing, and carrying on about something or other. I never saw such a bird for delivering opinions. Nothing escapes him; he notices everything that happens, and brings out his opinion about it, particularly if it is a matter that is none of his business. And it is never a mild opinion, but always violent—violent and profane—the presence of ladies does not affect him. His opinions are not the outcome of reflection, for he never thinks about anything, but heaves out the opinion that is on top in his mind, and which is often an opinion about some quite different thing and does not fit the case. But that is his way; his main idea is to get out an opinion, and if he stopped to think he would lose chances.

I suppose he has no enemies among men. The whites and Mohammedans never seemed to molest him; and the Hindus, because of their religion, never take the life of any creature, but spare even the snakes and tigers and fleas and rats. If I sat on one end of the balcony, the crows would gather on the railing at the other end and talk about me; and edge closer, little by little, till I could almost reach them; and they would sit there, in the most unabashed way, and talk about my clothes, and my hair, and my complexion, and probable character and vocation and politics, and how I came to be in India, and what I had been doing, and how many days I had got for it, and how I had happened to go unhanged so long, and when would it probably come off, and might there be more of my sort where I came from, and when would *they* be hanged—and so on, and so on, until I could not longer endure the embarrassment of it; then I would shoo them away, and they would circle around in the air a little while, laughing and deriding and mocking, and presently settle on the rail and do it all over again.

They were very sociable when there was anything to eat—oppressively so. With a little encouragement they would come in and light on the table and help me eat my breakfast; and once when I was in the other room and they found themselves alone, they carried off everything they could lift; and they were particular to choose things which they could make no use of after they got them. In India their number is beyond estimate, and their noise is in proportion. I suppose they cost the country more than the government does; yet that is not a light matter. Still, they pay; their company pays; it would sadden the land to take their cheerful voice out of it.

THE SHIFTY-EYED CHAMELEON

Everywhere he went, whether in America, Europe, the Mediterranean, or the Far East, Mark Twain found some counterpart of human nature in the animal kingdom. Birds and beasts—even the fish and insects—delighted him with their uniqueness and their idiosyncrasies, their single-mindedness and their self-containment. Harried by the domestic and business problems of a complicated human world, he must have envied the naturalness and simplicity of the animal world. Certain it is that Mark Twain, the humorist and social critic, often portrayed the birds and beasts in a satirical fashion, not to disparage them, but to expose the foibles of mankind. One of his last "fables," composed during his tour of South Africa, consummates his art. On this occasion the reader of Following the Equator *finds Mark Twain pausing outside the Royal Hotel in Durban to observe and describe the most efficient little creature he had ever encountered:*

The chameleon in the hotel court. He is fat and indolent and contemplative; but is businesslike and capable when a fly comes about—reaches out a tongue like a teaspoon and takes him in. He gums his tongue first. He is always pious, in his looks. And pious and thankful both, when Providence or one of us sends him a fly. He has a froggy head, and a back like a new grave—for shape; and hands like a bird's toes that have been frost-bitten. But his eyes are his exhibition feature. A couple of skinny cones project from the sides of his head, with a wee shiny bead of an eye set in the apex of each; and these cones turn bodily like pivot-guns and point every which way, and they are independent of each other; each has its own exclusive machinery. When I am behind him and C. in front of him, he whirls one eye rearward and the other forward—which gives him a most Congressional expression (one eye on the constituency and one on the swag); and then if something happens above and below him he shoots out one eye upward like a telescope and the other downward—and this changes his expression, but does not improve it.

4 · SOME ANIMAL TALES

One of the many wonders of Australia which prompted ex-tended commentary from Mark Twain was the most elemen-tal of sea creatures, the shark. "Sydney Harbor," he recorded, "is populous with the finest breeds of man-eating sharks in the world. Some people make their living catching them; for the Government pays a cash bounty on them. The larger the shark the larger the bounty, and some of the sharks are twenty feet long. You not only get the bounty, but everything that

84

is in the shark belongs to you. Sometimes the contents are quite valuable." Never one to miss a good opportunity to tell a story, the globe-trotting humorist used these factual obser-vations as the springboard for a story from Following the Equator *about one of the most colorful characters of the time:*

The shark is the swiftest fish that swims. The speed of the fastest steamer afloat is poor compared to his. And he is a great gad-about, and roams far and wide in the oceans, and visits the shores of all of them, ultimately, in the course of his restless excursions. I have a tale to tell now, which has not as yet been in print. In 1870 a young stranger arrived in Sydney, and set about finding something to do; but he knew no one, and brought no recommendations, and the result was that he got no employment. He had aimed high, at first, but as time and his money wasted away he grew less and less exacting, until at last he was willing to serve in the humblest capacities if so he might get bread and shelter. But luck was still against him; he could find no opening of any sort. Finally his money was all gone. He walked the streets all day, thinking; he walked them all night, thinking, thinking, and growing hungrier and hungrier. At dawn he found himself well away from the town and drifting aimlessly along the harbor shore. As he was pass-ing by a nodding shark-fisher the man looked up and said:

"Say, young fellow, take my line a spell, and change my luck for me."

"How do you know I won't make it worse?"

"Because you can't. It has been at its worst all night. If you can't change it, no harm's done; if you do change it, it's for the better, of course. Come."

"All right, what will you give?"

"I'll give you the shark, if you catch one."

"And I will eat it, bones and all. Give me the line."

"Here you are. I will get away, now, for a while, so that my luck won't spoil yours; for many and many a time I've noticed that if—there, pull in, pull in, man, you've got a bite! *I* knew how it would be. Why, I knew you for a born son of luck the minute I saw you. All right—he's landed."

It was an unusually large shark—"a full nineteen-footer," the fisherman said, as he laid the creature open with his knife.

"Now you rob him, young man, while I step to my hamper for a fresh bait. There's generally something in them worth going for. You've changed my luck, you see. But, my goodness, I hope you haven't changed your own."

"Oh, it wouldn't matter; don't worry about that. Get your bait. I'll rob him."

When the fisherman got back the young man had just finished washing his hands in the bay and was starting away.

"What! you are not going?"

"Yes. Good-bye."

"But what about your shark?"

"The shark? Why, what use is he to me?"

"What *use* is he? I like that. Don't you know that we can go and report him to Government, and you'll get a clean solid eighty shillings bounty? Hard cash, you know. What do you think about it *now*?"

"Oh, well, you can collect it."

"And *keep* it? Is that what you mean?"

"Yes."

"Well, this is odd. You're one of those sort they call eccentrics, I judge. The saying is, you mustn't judge a man by his clothes, and I'm believing it now. Why yours are looking just ratty, don't you know; and yet you must be rich."

"I am."

The young man walked slowly back to the town, deeply musing as he went. He halted a moment in front of the best restaurant, then glanced at his clothes and passed on, and got his breakfast at a "stand-up." There was a good deal of it, and it cost five shillings. He tendered a sovereign, got his change, glanced at his silver, muttered to himself, "There isn't enough to buy clothes with," and went his way.

At half past nine the richest wool-broker in Sydney was sitting in his morning-room at home, settling his breakfast with the morning paper. A servant put his head in and said:

"There's a sundowner at the door wants to see you, sir."

"What do you bring that kind of a message here for? Send him about his business."

"He won't go, sir. I've tried."

"He won't go? That's—why, that's unusual. He's one of two things, then: he's a remarkable person, or he's crazy. Is he crazy?"

"No, sir. He don't look it."

"Then he's remarkable. What does he say he wants?"

"He won't tell, sir; only says it's very important."

"And won't go. Does he *say* he won't go?"

"Says he'll stand there till he sees you, sir, if it's all day."

"And yet isn't crazy. Show him up."

The sundowner was shown in. The broker said to himself, "No, he's not crazy; that is easy to see; so he must be the other thing."

Then aloud, "Well, my good fellow, be quick about it; don't waste any words; what is it you want?"

"I want to borrow a hundred thousand pounds."

"Scott! (It's a mistake; he *is* crazy. . . . No—he *can't* be—not with that eye.) Why, you take my breath away. Come, who *are* you?"

"Nobody that you know."

"What is your name?"

"Cecil Rhodes."

"No, I don't remember hearing the name before. Now then—just for curiosity's sake—what has sent you to me on this extraordinary errand?"

"The intention to make a hundred thousand pounds for you and as much for myself within the next sixty days."

"Well, well, well. It is the most extraordinary idea that I—sit *down*—you interest me. And somehow you—well, you fascinate me, I think that that is about the word. And it isn't your proposition—no, that doesn't fascinate me; it's something else, I don't quite know what; something that's born in you and oozes out of you, I suppose. Now then—just for curiosity's sake again, nothing more: as I understand it, it is your desire to bor—"

"I said *intention*."

"Pardon, so you did. I thought it was an unheedful use of the word—an unheedful valuing of its strength, you know."

"I knew its strength."

"Well, I must say—but look here, let me walk the floor a little, my mind is getting into a sort of whirl, though *you* don't seem disturbed any. (Plainly this young fellow isn't crazy; but

88

as to his being remarkable—well, really he amounts to that, and something over.) Now then, I believe I am beyond the reach of further astonishment. Strike, and spare not. What is your scheme?"

"To buy the wool crop—deliverable in sixty days."

"What, the *whole* of it?"

"The whole of it."

"No, I was not quite out of the reach of surprises, after all. Why, how you talk. Do you know what our crop is going to foot up?"

"Two and a half million sterling—maybe a little more."

"Well, you've got your statistics right, anyway. Now then, do you know what the margins would foot up, to buy it at sixty days?"

"The hundred thousand pounds I came here to get."

"Right, once more. Well, dear me, just to see what would happen, I wish you had the money. And if you had it, what would you do with it?"

"I shall make two hundred thousand pounds out of it in sixty days."

"You mean, of course, that you *might* make it if—"

"I said 'shall.' "

"Yes, by George, you *did* say 'shall'! You are the most definite devil I ever saw, in the matter of language. Dear, dear, dear, look here! Definite speech means clarity of mind. Upon my word I believe you've got what you believe to be a rational *reason* for venturing into this house, an entire stranger, on this wild scheme of buying the wool crop of an entire colony on speculation. Bring it out—I am prepared—acclimatized, if I may use the word. *Why* would you buy the crop, and *why* would you make that sum out of it? That is to say, what makes you think you—"

"I don't think—I know."

"Definite again. *How* do you know?"

"Because France has declared war against Germany, and wool has gone up fourteen per cent. in London and is still rising."

"Oh, in-deed? *Now* then, I've *got* you! Such a thunderbolt as you have just let fly ought to have made me jump out of my chair, but it didn't stir me the least little bit, you see. And for a very simple reason: I have read the morning paper. You can look at it if you want to. The fastest ship in the service arrived at eleven o'clock last night, fifty days out from London. All her news is printed here. There are no war-clouds anywhere; and as for wool, why, it is the low-spiritedest commodity in the English market. It is your turn to jump, now.... Well, why don't you jump? Why do you sit there in that placid fashion, when—"

"Because I have later news."

"Later news? Oh, come—later news than fifty days, brought steaming hot from London by the—"

"My news is only ten days old."

"Oh, Mun-*chausen*, hear the maniac talk! Where did you get it?"

"Got it out of a shark."

"Oh, oh, oh, this is *too* much! Front! call the police—bring the gun—raise the town! All the asylums in Christendom have broken loose in the single person of—"

"Sit down! And collect yourself. Where is the use in getting excited? Am I excited? There is nothing to get excited *about*. When I make a statement which I cannot prove, it will be time enough for you to begin to offer hospitality to damaging fancies about me and my sanity."

"Oh, a thousand thousand pardons! I ought to be ashamed of myself, and I *am* ashamed of myself for thinking that a little bit of a circumstance like sending a shark to England to fetch back a market report—"

"What does your middle initial stand for, sir?"

"Andrew. What are you writing?"

"Wait a moment. Proof about the shark—and another matter. Only ten lines. There—now it is done. Sign it."

"Many thanks—many. Let me see; it says—it says—oh, come, this is *interesting*! Why—why—look here! prove what you say here, and I'll put up the money, and double as much, if necessary, and divide the winnings with you, half and half. There, now—I've signed; make your promise good if you can. Show me a copy of the London *Times* only ten days old."

"Here it is—and with it these buttons and a memorandum-book that belonged to the man the shark swallowed. Swallowed him in the Thames, without a doubt; for you will notice that the last entry in the book is dated 'London,' and is of the same date as the *Times*, and says 'As a consequence of the declaration of war, I journey today to the Fatherland, that I may lay my life on the altar of my country' [translated]—as clean native German as anybody can put upon paper, and means that in consequence of the declaration of war, this loyal soul is leaving for home *to-day*, to fight. And he did leave, too, but the shark had him before the day was done, poor fellow."

"And a pity, too. But there are times for mourning, and

we will attend to this case further on; other matters are pressing, now. I will go down and set the machinery in motion in a quiet way and buy the crop. It will cheer the drooping spirits of the boys, in a transitory way. Everything is transitory in this world. Sixty days hence, when they are called to deliver the goods, they will think they've been struck by lightning. But there is a time for mourning, and we will attend to that case along with the other one. Come along, I'll take you to my tailor. What did you say your name is?"

"Cecil Rhodes."

"It is hard to remember. However, I think you will make it easier by and by, if you live. There are three kinds of people —Commonplace Men, Remarkable Men, and Lunatics. I'll classify you with the Remarkables, and take the chances."

The deal went through, and secured to the young stranger the first fortune he ever pocketed.

A DOG'S TALE

The reader will immediately see certain differences between Mark Twain's earlier animal sketches and tales and the two stories that follow. "A Dog's Tale" and "A Horse's Tale" were written during their author's last years, when he was a wiser but sadder man; and he wrote each story with a kind of "social purpose": to protest against cruelty to animals.

In his earlier writing about animals, Mark Twain had portrayed his creatures as only an outside observer would see them, and he had used most of his animal portraits simply as anecdotes in a larger account. But in these last two stories he assumes the role of the animal itself and lets the animal give an account of its complete life. Thus these stories become

*animal autobiographies, revealing the innermost thoughts and
feelings of their subjects. If dogs and horses have thoughts and
feelings, Mark Twain would say, the only possible way to
express them is to let these creatures tell their own stories. This
may be a less "realistic" view of animals, but it is a more
imaginative and therefore a more appealing approach to the
animal world. If we do not actually see the dog and the horse
of these two stories as well as we saw the cats, the dogs, the
horses, the frog, and other animalia of Mark Twain's early
writing, at least we* understand *them better. And it is only
through better understanding, implies the author, that man
can come to love his fellow creatures and learn to treat them
with the kindness and respect they deserve.*

My father was a St. Bernard, my mother was a collie, but I
am a Presbyterian. This is what my mother told me; I do not
know these nice distinctions myself. To me they are only fine
large words meaning nothing. My mother had a fondness for
such; she liked to say them, and see other dogs look surprised
and envious, as wondering how she got so much education.
But, indeed, it was not real education; it was only show: she
got the words by listening in the dining-room and drawing-
room when there was company, and by going with the children to Sunday-school and listening there; and whenever she
heard a large word she said it over to herself many times, and
so was able to keep it until there was a dogmatic gathering in
the neighborhood, then she would get it off, and surprise and
distress them all, from pocket-pup to mastiff, which rewarded
her for all her trouble. If there was a stranger he was nearly
sure to be suspicious, and when he got his breath again he

would ask her what it meant. And she always told him. He was never expecting this, but thought he would catch her; so when she told him, he was the one that looked ashamed, whereas he had thought it was going to be she. The others were always waiting for this, and glad of it and proud of her, for they knew what was going to happen, because they had had experience. When she told the meaning of a big word they were all so taken up with admiration that it never occurred to any dog to doubt if it was the right one; and that was natural, because, for one thing, she answered up so promptly that it seemed like a dictionary speaking, and for another thing, where could they find out whether it was right or not? for she was the only cultivated dog there was. By and by, when I was older, she brought home the word Unintellectual, one time, and worked it pretty hard all the week at different gatherings, making much unhappiness and despondency; and it was at this time that I noticed that during that week she was asked for the meaning at eight different assemblages, and flashed out a fresh definition every time, which showed me that she had more presence of mind than culture, though I said nothing, of course. She had one word which she always kept on hand, and ready, like a life-preserver, a kind of emergency word to strap on when she was likely to get washed overboard in a sudden way—that was the word Synonymous. When she happened to fetch out a long word which had had its day weeks before and its prepared meanings gone to her dump-pile, if there was a stranger there of course it knocked him groggy for a couple of minutes, then he would come to, and by that time she would be away down the wind on another tack, and not expecting anything; so

94

when he'd hail and ask her to cash in, I (the only dog on the inside of her game) could see her canvas flicker a moment—but only just a moment—then it would belly out taut and full, and she would say, as calm as a summer's day, "It's synonymous with supererogation," or some godless long reptile of a word like that, and go placidly about and skim away on the next tack, perfectly comfortable, you know, and leave that stranger looking profane and embarrassed, and the initiated slatting the floor with their tails in unison and their faces transfigured with a holy joy.

And it was the same with phrases. She would drag home a whole phrase, if it had a grand sound, and play it six nights and two matinées, and explain it a new way every time—which she had to, for all she cared for was the phrase; she wasn't interested in what it meant, and knew those dogs hadn't wit enough to catch her, anyway. Yes, she was a daisy! She got so she wasn't afraid of anything, she had such confidence in the ignorance of those creatures. She even brought anecdotes that she had heard the family and the dinner-guests laugh and shout over; and as a rule she got the nub of one chestnut hitched onto another chestnut, where, of course, it didn't fit and hadn't any point; and when she delivered the nub she fell over and rolled on the floor and laughed and barked in the most insane way, while I could see that she was wondering to herself why it didn't seem as funny as it did when she first heard it. But no harm was done; the others rolled and barked too, privately ashamed of themselves for not seeing the point, and never suspecting that the fault was not with them and there wasn't any to see.

You can see by these things that she was of a rather vain

95

and frivolous character; still, she had virtues, and enough to make up, I think. She had a kind heart and gentle ways, and never harbored resentments for injuries done her, but put them easily out of her mind and forgot them; and she taught her children her kindly way, and from her we learned also to be brave and prompt in time of danger, and not to run away, but face the peril that threatened friend or stranger, and help him the best we could without stopping to think what the cost might be to us. And she taught us not by words only, but by example, and that is the best way and the surest and the most lasting. Why, the brave things she did, the splendid things! she was just a soldier; and so modest about it—well, you couldn't help admiring her, and you couldn't help imitating her; not even a King Charles spaniel could remain entirely despicable in her society. So, as you see, there was more to her than her education.

When I was well grown, at last, I was sold and taken away, and I never saw her again. She was broken-hearted, and so was I, and we cried; but she comforted me as well as she could, and said we were sent into this world for a wise and good purpose, and must do our duties without repining, take our life as we might find it, live it for the best good of others, and never mind about the results; they were not our affair. She said men who did like this would have a noble and beautiful reward by and by in another world, and although we animals would not go there, to do well and right without reward would give to our brief lives a worthiness and dignity which in itself would be a reward. She had gathered these things from time to time when she had gone to the Sunday-school with the children, and had laid them up in her memory more carefully than she had done with those other words and phrases; and she had studied them deeply, for her good and ours. One may see by this that she had a wise and thoughtful head, for all there was so much lightness and vanity in it.

So we said our farewells, and looked our last upon each other through our tears; and the last thing she said—keeping it for the last to make me remember it the better, I think— was, "In memory of me, when there is a time of danger to another do not think of yourself, think of your mother, and do as she would do."

Do you think I could forget that? No.

It was such a charming home!—my new one; a fine great house, with pictures, and delicate decorations, and rich furni- ture, and no gloom anywhere, but all the wilderness of dainty colors lit up with flooding sunshine; and the spacious grounds around it, and the great garden—oh, greensward, and noble trees, and flowers, no end! And I was the same as a member of the family; and they loved me, and petted me, and did not give me a new name, but called me by my old one that was dear to me because my mother had given it me—Aileen Mavourneen. She got it out of a song; and the Grays knew that song, and said it was a beautiful name.

Mrs. Gray was thirty, and so sweet and so lovely, you can- not imagine it; and Sadie was ten, and just like her mother, just a darling slender little copy of her, with auburn tails down her back, and short frocks; and the baby was a year old, and plump and dimpled, and fond of me, and never could get enough of hauling on my tail, and hugging me, and laughing out its innocent happiness; and Mr. Gray was thirty-eight, and tall and slender and handsome, a little bald in front, alert, quick in his movements, business-like, prompt, decided, unsentimental, and with that kind of trim-chiseled face that just seems to glint and sparkle with frosty intellectuality! He was a renowned scientist. I do not know what the word means, but my mother would know how to use it and get effects. She would know how to depress a rat-terrier with it and make a lap-dog look sorry he came. But that is not the best one; the best one was Laboratory. My mother could organize a Trust on that one that would skin the tax-collars off the whole herd. The laboratory was not a book, or a picture, or a place to wash your hands in, as the college president's dog said—no, that is the lavatory; the laboratory is quite different, and is filled with jars, and bottles, and electrics, and wires, and strange machines; and every week other scientists came there and sat in the place, and used the machines, and discussed, and made what they called experiments and discoveries; and often I came, too, and stood around and listened, and tried to learn, for the sake of my mother, and in loving memory of her, although it was a pain to me, as realizing what she was losing out of her life and I gaining nothing at all; for try as I might, I was never able to make anything out of it at all.

Other times I lay on the floor in the mistress's work-room and slept, she gently using me for a foot-stool, knowing it pleased me, for it was a caress; other times I spent an hour in the nursery, and got well tousled and made happy; other times I watched by the crib there, when the baby was asleep and the nurse out for a few minutes on the baby's affairs; other times I romped and raced through the grounds and the garden with Sadie till we were tired out, then slumbered on the grass in the shade of a tree while she read her book; other times I went visiting among the neighbor dogs—for there were some most pleasant ones not far away, and one very handsome and courteous and graceful one, a curly-haired Irish setter by the name of Robin Adair, who was a Presbyterian like me, and belonged to the Scotch minister.

The servants in our house were all kind to me and were fond of me, and so, as you see, mine was a pleasant life. There could not be a happier dog than I was, nor a gratefuller one. I will say this for myself, for it is only the truth: I tried in all ways to do well and right, and honor my mother's memory and her teachings, and earn the happiness that had come to me, as best I could.

By and by came my little puppy, and then my cup was full, my happiness was perfect. It was the dearest little waddling thing, and so smooth and soft and velvety, and had such cunning little awkward paws, and such affectionate eyes, and such a sweet and innocent face; and it made me so proud to see how the children and their mother adored it, and fondled it, and exclaimed over every little wonderful thing it did. It did seem to me that life was just too lovely to—

Then came the winter. One day I was standing a watch in the nursery. That is to say, I was asleep on the bed. The baby was asleep in the crib, which was alongside the bed, on the side next the fireplace. It was the kind of crib that has a lofty tent over it made of a gauzy stuff that you can see through. The nurse was out, and we two sleepers were alone. A spark from the wood-fire was shot out, and it lit on the slope of the tent. I suppose a quiet interval followed, then a scream from the

99

baby woke me, and there was that tent flaming up toward the ceiling! Before I could think, I sprang to the floor in my fright, and in a second was half-way to the door; but in the next half-second my mother's farewell was sounding in my ears, and I was back on the bed again. I reached my head through the flames and dragged the baby out by the waistband, and tugged it along, and we fell to the floor together in a cloud of smoke; I snatched a new hold, and dragged the screaming little creature along and out at the door and around the bend of the hall, and was still tugging away, all excited and happy and proud, when the master's voice shouted:

"Begone, you cursed beast!" and I jumped to save myself; but he was wonderfully quick, and chased me up, striking furiously at me with his cane, I dodging this way and that, in terror, and at last a strong blow fell upon my left foreleg, which made me shriek and fall, for the moment, helpless; the cane went up for another blow, but never descended, for the nurse's voice rang wildly out, "The nursery's on fire!" and the master rushed away in that direction, and my other bones were saved.

The pain was cruel, but, no matter, I must not lose any time; he might come back at any moment; so I limped on three legs to the other end of the hall, where there was a dark little stairway leading up into a garret where old boxes and such things were kept, as I had heard say, and where people seldom went. I managed to climb up there, then I searched my way through the dark among the piles of things, and hid in the secretest place I could find. It was foolish to be afraid there, yet still I was; so afraid that I held in and hardly even whimpered, though it would have been such a comfort to whimper, because that eases the pain, you know. But I could lick my leg, and that did me some good.

For half an hour there was a commotion downstairs, and shoutings, and rushing footsteps, and then there was quiet again. Quiet for some minutes, and that was grateful to my spirit, for then my fears began to go down; and fears are worse than pains—oh, much worse. Then came a sound that froze me. They were calling me—calling me by name—hunting for me!

It was muffled by distance, but that could not take the terror out of it, and it was the most dreadful sound to me that I had ever heard. It went all about, everywhere, down there: along the halls, through all the rooms, in both stories, and in the basement and the cellar; then outside, and farther and farther away—then back, and all about the house again, and I thought it would never, never stop. But at last it did, hours and hours after the vague twilight of the garret had long ago been blotted out by black darkness.

Then in that blessed stillness my terrors fell little by little away, and I was at peace and slept. It was a good rest I had, but I woke before the twilight had come again. I was feeling fairly comfortable, and I could think out a plan now. I made a very good one; which was, to creep down, all the way down the back stairs, and hide behind the cellar door, and slip out and escape when the iceman came at dawn, while he was inside filling the refrigerator; then I would hide all day, and start on my journey when night came; my journey to—well, anywhere where they would not know me and betray me to the master. I was feeling almost cheerful now; then suddenly I thought: Why, what would life be without my puppy!

That was despair. There was no plan for me; I saw that; I must stay where I was; stay, and wait, and take what might come—it was not my affair; that was what life is—my mother had said it. Then—well, then the calling began again! All my sorrows came back. I said to myself, the master will never forgive. I did not know what I had done to make him so bitter and so unforgiving, yet I judged it was something a dog could not understand, but which was clear to a man and dreadful.

They called and called—days and nights, it seemed to me. So long that the hunger and thirst near drove me mad, and I recognized that I was getting very weak. When you are this way you sleep a great deal, and I did. Once I woke in an awful fright—it seemed to me that the calling was right there in the garret! And so it was: it was Sadie's voice, and she was crying; my name was falling from her lips all broken, poor thing, and I could not believe my ears for the joy of it when I heard her say:

"Come back to us—oh, come back to us, and forgive—it is all so sad without our—"

I broke in with *such* a grateful little yelp, and the next moment Sadie was plunging and stumbling through the darkness and the lumber and shouting for the family to hear, "She's found! she's found!"

The days that followed—well, they were wonderful. The mother and Sadie and the servants—why, they just seemed to worship me. They couldn't seem to make me a bed that was fine enough; and as for food, they couldn't be satisfied with anything but game and delicacies that were out of season; and every day the friends and neighbors flocked in to hear about my heroism—that was the name they called it by, and it means agriculture. I remember my mother pulling it on a kennel once, and explaining it that way, but didn't say what agriculture was, except that it was synonymous with intramural incandescence; and a dozen times a day Mrs. Gray and Sadie would tell the tale to new-comers, and say I risked my life to save the baby's, and both of us had burns to prove it, and then the company would pass me around and pet me and exclaim about me, and you could see the pride in the eyes of Sadie and her mother; and when the people wanted to know what made me limp, they looked ashamed and changed the subject, and sometimes when people hunted them this way and that way with questions about it, it looked to me as if they were going to cry.

And this was not all the glory; no, the master's friends came, a whole twenty of the most distinguished people, and had me in the laboratory, and discussed me as if I was a kind of discovery; and some of them said it was wonderful in a dumb beast, the finest exhibition of instinct they could call to mind; but the master said, with vehemence, "It's far above instinct; it's *reason*, and many a man, privileged to be saved and go with you and me to a better world by right of its possession, has less of it than this poor silly quadruped that's fore-ordained to perish"; and then he laughed, and said: "Why, look at me—I'm a sarcasm! bless you, with all my grand intelligence, the only thing I inferred was that the dog had gone mad and was destroying the child, whereas but for the beast's intelligence—it's *reason*, I tell you!—the child would have perished!"

They disputed and disputed, and *I* was the very center and subject of it all, and I wished my mother could know that this grand honor had come to me; it would have made her proud.

Then they discussed optics, as they called it, and whether a certain injury to the brain would produce blindness or not, but they could not agree about it, and said they must test it by experiment by and by; and next they discussed plants, and that interested me, because in the summer Sadie and I had planted seeds—I helped her dig the holes, you know—and after days and days a little shrub or a flower came up there, and it was a wonder how that could happen; but it did, and I wished I could talk—I would have told those people about it and shown them how much I knew, and been all alive with the subject; but I didn't care for the optics; it was dull, and when they came back to it again it bored me, and I went to sleep.

Pretty soon it was spring, and sunny and pleasant and lovely, and the sweet mother and the children patted me and the puppy good-by, and went away on a journey and a visit to their kin, and the master wasn't any company for us, but we played together and had good times, and the servants were kind and friendly, so we got along quite happily and counted the days and waited for the family.

And one day those men came again, and said, now for the test, and they took the puppy to the laboratory, and I limped three-leggedly along, too, feeling proud, for any attention shown the puppy was a pleasure to me, of course. They discussed and experimented, and then suddenly the puppy shrieked, and they set him on the floor, and he went staggering around, with his head all bloody, and the master clapped his hands and shouted:

"There, I've won—confess it! He's as blind as a bat!"

And they all said:

"It's so—you've proved your theory, and suffering human-ity owes you a great debt from henceforth," and they crowded around him, and wrung his hand cordially and thankfully, and praised him.

But I hardly saw or heard these things, for I ran at once to my little darling, and snuggled close to it where it lay, and licked the blood, and it put its head against mine, whimpering softly, and I knew in my heart it was a comfort to it in its pain and trouble to feel its mother's touch, though it could not see me. Then it dropped down, presently, and its little velvet nose rested upon the floor, and it was still, and did not move any more.

Soon the master stopped discussing a moment, and rang in the footman, and said, "Bury it in the far corner of the garden," and then went on with the discussion, and I trotted after the footman, very happy and grateful, for I knew the puppy was out of its pain now, because it was asleep. We went far down the garden to the farthest end, where the children and the nurse and the puppy and I used to play in the summer in the shade of a great elm, and there the footman dug a hole, and I saw he was going to plant the puppy, and I was glad, because it would grow and come up a fine handsome dog, like Robin Adair, and be a beautiful surprise for the family when they came home; so I tried to help him dig, but my lame leg was no good, being stiff, you know, and you have to have two, or it is no use. When the footman had finished and covered little Robin up, he patted my head, and there were tears in his eyes, and he said: "Poor little doggie, you SAVED *his* child."

I have watched two whole weeks, and he doesn't come up! This last week a fright has been stealing upon me. I think there is something terrible about this. I do not know what it is, but the fear makes me sick, and I cannot eat, though the servants bring me the best of food; and they pet me so, and even come in the night, and cry, and say, "Poor doggie—do give it up and come home; *don't* break our hearts!" and all this terrifies me the more, and makes me sure something has happened. And I am so weak; since yesterday I cannot stand on my feet any more. And within this hour the servants, looking toward the sun where it was sinking out of sight and the night chill coming on said things I could not understand but they carried something cold to my heart.

"Those poor creatures! They do not suspect. They will come home in the morning, and eagerly ask for the little doggie that did the brave deed, and who of us will be strong enough to say the truth to them: " 'The humble little friend is gone where go the beasts that perish.' "

A HORSE'S TALE

In his Mark Twain: A Biography, *Albert Bigelow Paine tells us that "A Horse's Tale" was originally planned to oblige Mrs. Minnie Maddern Fiske, to aid her in a crusade against bullfighting in Spain. "I have lain awake nights," she wrote Mark Twain, "wondering if I dare to ask you to write a story of an old horse that is finally given over to the bull-ring. The story you would write would do more than all the laws we are trying to have made and enforced for the prevention of cruelty to animals in Spain. We would translate and circulate* it in that country." To which Mark Twain replied, "I shall certainly write the story."

The result of Mrs. Fiske's request is a sentimental tale about the favorite horse of Buffalo Bill. A little Spanish girl wins the hearts of both the man and the horse, and when she returns to Spain it is inevitable that the horse, Soldier Boy, be taken with her. Soldier Boy is kidnapped, treated infamously, and finally, a broken wreck, sent to the bull-ring. He is killed by the bull, but just before his death the little Spanish girl recognizes him and runs to him in the ring, where she also is killed.

One chapter in the long story is rather exceptional in that it contains much more of the humor which is Mark Twain's forte than is found in the rest. This episode, a conversation between two horses, takes place while Soldier Boy and the little girl are still on an army post in western America:

SOLDIER BOY AND THE MEXICAN PLUG

"When did you come?" [Soldier Boy.]

"Arrived at sundown." [Mexican Plug.]

"Where from?"

"Salt Lake."

"Are you in the service?"

"No. Trade."

"Pirate trade, I reckon."

"What do you know about it?"

"I saw you when you came. I recognized your master. He is a bad sort. Trap-robber, horse-thief, squaw-man, renegado—Hank Butters—I know him very well. Stole you, didn't he?"

"Well, it amounted to that."

"I thought so. Where is his pard?"

"He stopped at White Cloud's camp."

"He is another of the same stripe, is Blake Haskins."
(*Aside.*) They are laying for Buffalo Bill again, I guess.
(*Aloud.*) "What is your name?"

"Which one?"

"Have you got more than one?"

"I get a new one every time I'm stolen. I used to have an
honest name, but that was early; I've forgotten it. Since then
I've had thirteen *aliases*."

"Aliases? What is alias?"

"A false name."

"Alias. It's a fine large word, and is in my line; it has quite
a learned and cerebrospinal incandescent sound. Are you
educated?"

"Well, no, I can't claim it. I can take down bars, I can dis-
tinguish oats from shoe-pegs, I can blaspheme a saddle-boil
with the college-bred, and I know a few other things—not
many; I have had no chance, I have always had to work;
besides, I am of low birth and no family. You speak my dialect
like a native, but you are not a Mexican Plug, you are a gentleman, I·can see that; and educated, of course."

"Yes, I am of old family, and not illiterate. I am a fossil."

"A which?"

"Fossil. The first horses were fossils. They date back two
million years."

"Gr-eat sand and sage-brush! do you mean it?"

"Yes, it is true. The bones of my ancestors are held in
reverence and worship, even by men. They do not leave them

exposed to the weather when they find them, but carry them three thousand miles and enshrine them in their temples of learning, and worship them."

"It is wonderful! I knew you must be a person of distinction, by your fine presence and courtly address, and by the fact that you are not subjected to the indignity of hobbles, like myself and the rest. Would you tell me your name?"

"You have probably heard of it—Soldier Boy."

"What!—the renowned, the illustrious?"

"Even so."

"It takes my breath! Little did I dream that ever I should stand face to face with the possessor of that great name. Buffalo Bill's horse! Known from the Canadian border to the deserts of Arizona, and from the eastern marches of the Great Plains to the foothills of the Sierra! Truly this is a memorable day. You still serve the celebrated Chief of Scouts?"

"I am still his property, but he has lent me, for a time, to the most noble, the most gracious, the most excellent, her Excellency Catherine, Corporal-General Seventh Cavalry and Flag-Lieutenant Ninth Dragoons, U. S. A.,—on whom be peace!"

"Amen. Did you say *her* Excellency?"

"The same. A Spanish lady, sweet blossom of a ducal house. And truly a wonder; knowing everything, capable of everything; speaking all the languages, master of all sciences, a mind without horizons, a heart of gold, the glory of her race! On whom be peace!"

"Amen. It is marvelous!"

"Verily. I knew many things, she has taught me others. I am educated. I will tell you about her."

"I listen—I am enchanted."

"I will tell a plain tale, calmly, without excitement, without eloquence. When she had been here four or five weeks she was already erudite in military things, and they made her an officer—a double officer. She rode the drill every day, like any soldier; and she could take the bugle and direct the evolutions herself. Then, on a day, there was a grand race, for prizes— none to enter but the children. Seventeen children entered, and she was the youngest. Three girls, fourteen boys—good riders all. It was a steeplechase, with four hurdles, all pretty high. The first prize was a most cunning half-grown silver bugle, and mighty pretty, with red silk cord and tassels. Buffalo Bill was very anxious; for he had taught her to ride, and he did most dearly want her to win that race, for the glory of it. So he wanted her to ride me, but she wouldn't; and she reproached him, and said it was unfair and unright, and taking advantage; for what horse in this post or any other could stand a chance against me? and she was very severe with him, and said, 'You ought to be ashamed—you are proposing to me conduct unbecoming an officer and a gentleman.' So he just tossed her up in the air about thirty feet and caught her as she came down, and said he *was* ashamed; and put up his handkerchief and pretended to cry, which nearly broke her heart, and she petted him, and begged him to forgive her, and said she would do anything in the world he could ask but that; but he said he ought to go hang himself, and he *must*, if he could get a rope; it was nothing but right he should, for he never, never could forgive himself; and then *she* began to cry, and they both sobbed, the way you could hear him a mile, and she clinging around his neck and pleading, till at last he was comforted a little, and gave his solemn promise he wouldn't hang himself till after the race; and wouldn't do it at all if she won it, which made her happy, and she said she would win it or die in the saddle; so then everything was pleasant again and both of them content. He can't help playing jokes on her, he is so fond of her and she is so innocent and unsuspecting; and when she finds it out she cuffs him and is in a fury, but presently forgives him because it's *him*; and maybe the very next day she's caught with another joke; you see she can't learn any better, because she hasn't any deceit in her, and that kind aren't ever expecting it in another person.

"It was a grand race. The whole post was there, and there was such another whooping and shouting when the seventeen kids came flying down the turf and sailing over the hurdles— oh, beautiful to see! Half-way down, it was kind of neck and neck, and anybody's race and nobody's. Then, what should happen but a cow steps out and puts her head down to munch grass, with her broadside to the battalion, and they a-coming like the wind; they split apart to flank her, but *she?*—why, she drove the spurs home and soared over that cow like a bird! and on she went, and cleared the last hurdle solitary and alone, the army letting loose the grand yell, and she skipped from the horse the same as if he had been standing still, and made her bow, and everybody crowded around to congratulate, and they gave her the bugle, and she put it to her lips and blew 'boots and saddles' to see how it would go, and BB was as proud as you can't think! And he said, 'Take Soldier Boy, and don't pass him back till I ask for him!' and I can tell you he wouldn't have said that to any other person on this planet. That was two months and more ago, and nobody has been on my back since but the Corporal-General Seventh Cavalry and Flag-Lieutenant of the Ninth Dragoons, U.S.A.,—on whom be peace!"

"Amen. I listen—tell me more."

"She set to work and organized the Sixteen, and called it the First Battalion Rocky Mountain Rangers, U.S.A., and she wanted to be bugler, but they elected her Lieutenant-General *and* Bugler. So she ranks her uncle the commandant, who is only a Brigadier. And doesn't she train those little people! Ask the Indians, ask the traders, ask the soldiers; they'll tell you. She has been at it from the first day. Every morning they go clattering down into the plain, and there she sits on my back with her bugle at her mouth and sounds the orders and puts them through the evolutions for an hour or more; and it is too beautiful for anything to see those ponies dissolve from one formation into another, and waltz about, and break, and scatter, and form again, always moving, always graceful, now trotting, now galloping, and so on, sometimes near by, sometimes in the distance, all just like a state ball, you know, and sometimes she can't hold herself any longer, but sounds the 'charge,' and turns me loose! and you can take my word for it, if the battalion hasn't *too* much of a start we catch up and go over the breastworks with the front line.

"Yes, they are soldiers, those little people; and healthy, too, not ailing any more, the way they used to be sometimes. It's because of her drill. She's got a fort, now—Fort Fanny Marsh. Major-General Tommy Drake planned it out, and the Seventh and Dragoons built it. Tommy is the Colonel's son, and is fifteen and the oldest in the Battalion; Fanny Marsh is Brigadier-General, and is next oldest—over thirteen. She is daughter of Captain Marsh, Company B, Seventh Cavalry. Lieutenant-General Alison is the youngest by considerable; I think she is about nine and a half or three-quarters. Her military rig, as Lieutenant-General, isn't for business, it's for dress parade, because the ladies made it. They say they got it out of the Middle Ages—out of a book—and it is all red and blue and white silks and satins and velvets; tights, trunks, sword, doublet with slashed sleeves, short cape, cap with just one feather in it; I've heard them name these things; they got them out of the book; she's dressed like a page, of old times, they say. It's the daintiest outfit that ever was—you will say so, when you see it. She's lovely in it—oh, just a dream! In some ways she is just her age, but in others she's as old as her uncle, I think. She is very learned. She teaches her uncle his book. I have seen her sitting by with the book and reciting to him what is in it, so that he can learn to do it himself.

"Every Saturday she hires little Injuns to garrison her fort; then she lays siege to it, and makes military approaches by make-believe trenches in make-believe night, and finally at make-believe dawn she draws her sword and sounds the assault and takes it by storm. It is for practice. And she has invented a bugle-call all by herself, out of her own head, and it's a stirring one, and the prettiest in the service. It's to call me—it's never used for anything else. She taught it to me, and told me what it says: '*It is I, Soldier—come!*' and when those thrilling notes come floating down the distance I hear them without fail, even if I am two miles away; and then—oh, then you should see my heels get down to business!

"And she has taught me how to say good-morning and good-night to her, which is by lifting my right hoof for her to shake; and also how to say good-by; I do that with my left foot—but only for practice, because there hasn't been any but make-believe good-bying yet, and I hope there won't ever be. It would make me cry if I ever had to put up my left foot in earnest. She has taught me how to salute, and I can do it as well as a soldier. I bow my head low, and lay my right hoof against my cheek. She taught me that because I got into disgrace once, through ignorance. I am privileged, because I am known to be honorable and trustworthy, and because I have a distinguished record in the service; so they don't hobble me nor tie me to stakes or shut me tight in stables, but let me wander around to suit myself. Well, trooping the colors is a very solemn ceremony, and everybody must stand uncovered when the flag goes by, the commandant and all; and once I was there, and ignorantly walked across right in front of the band, which was an awful disgrace. Ah, the Lieutenant-General was so ashamed, and so distressed that I should have done such a thing before all the world, that she couldn't keep the tears back; and then she taught me the salute, so that if I ever did any other unmilitary act through ignorance I could do my salute and she believed everybody would think it was apology enough and would not press the matter. It is very nice and distinguished; no other horse can do it; often the men salute me, and I return it. I am privileged to be present when the Rocky Mountain Rangers troop the colors and I stand solemn, like the children, and I salute when the flag goes by. Of course when she goes to her fort her sentries sing out 'Turn out the guard!' and then ... do you catch that refreshing early-morning whiff from the mountain-pines and the wild flowers? The night is far spent; we'll hear the bugles before long. Dorcas, the black woman, is very good and nice; she takes care of the Lieutenant-General, and is Brigadier-General Alison's mother, which makes her mother-in-law to the Lieutenant-General. That is what Shekels says. At least it is what I think he says, though I never can understand him quite clearly. He—"

"Who is Shekels?"

"The Seventh Cavalry dog. I mean, if he *is* a dog. His father was a coyote and his mother was a wild-cat. It doesn't really make a dog out of him, does it?"

"Not a real dog, I should think. Only a kind of a general dog, at most, I reckon. Though this is a matter of ichthyology, I suppose; and if it is, it is out of my depth, and so my opinion is not valuable, and I don't claim much consideration for it."

"It isn't ichthyology; it is dogmatics, which is still more difficult and tangled up. Dogmatics always are."

"Dogmatics is quite beyond me, quite; so I am not competing. But on general principles it is my opinion that a colt out of a coyote and a wild-cat is no square dog, but doubtful. That is my hand, and I stand pat."

"Well, it is as far as I can go myself, and be fair and conscientious. I have always regarded him as a doubtful dog, and so has Potter. Potter is the great Dane. Potter says he is no dog, and not even poultry—though I do not go quite so far as that."

"And I wouldn't, myself. Poultry is one of those things which no person can get to the bottom of, there is so much of it and such variety. It is just wings, and wings, and wings, till you are weary; turkeys, and geese, and bats, and butterflies, and angels, and grasshoppers, and flying-fish, and—well, there is really no end to the tribe; it gives me the heaves just to think of it. But this one hasn't any wings, has he?"

"No."

"Well, then, in my belief he is more likely to be dog than poultry. I have not heard of poultry that hadn't wings. Wings is the *sign* of poultry; it is what you tell poultry by. Look at the mosquito."

"What do you reckon he is, then? He must be something."

"Why, he could be a reptile; anything that hasn't wings is a reptile."

"Who told you that?"

"Nobody told me, but I overheard it."

"Where did you overhear it?"

"Years ago. I was with the Philadelphia Institute expedition in the Bad Lands under Professor Cope, hunting mastodon bones, and I overheard him say, his own self, that any plantigrade circumflex vertebrate bacterium that hadn't wings and was uncertain was a reptile. Well, then, has this dog any wings? No. Is he a plantigrade circumflex vertebrate bacterium? Maybe so, maybe not; but without ever having seen him, and judging only by his illegal and spectacular parentage, I will bet the odds of a bale of hay to a bran mash that he looks it. Finally, is he uncertain? That is the point—is he uncertain? I will leave it to you if you have ever heard of a more uncertainer dog than what this one is?"

"No, I never have."

"Well, then, he's a reptile. That's settled."

"Why, look here, whatsyourname—"

"Last alias, Mongrel."

"A good one, too. I was going to say, you are better educated than you have been pretending to be. I like cultured society, and I shall cultivate your acquaintance. Now as to Shekels, whenever you want to know about any private thing that is going on at this post or in White Cloud's camp or Thunder-Bird's, he can tell you; and if you make friends with him he'll be glad to, for he is a born gossip, and picks up all the tittle-tattle. Being the whole Seventh Cavalry's reptile, he doesn't belong to anybody in particular, and hasn't any military duties; so he comes and goes as he pleases, and is popular with all the house cats and other authentic sources of private information. He understands all the languages, and talks them all, too. With an accent like gritting your teeth, it is true, and with a grammar that is no improvement on blasphemy—still, with practice you get at the meat of what he says, and it serves.... Hark! That's the reveille....

"Faint and far, but isn't it clear, isn't it sweet? There's no music like the bugle to stir the blood, in the still solemnity of the morning twilight, with the dim plain stretching away to nothing and the spectral mountains slumbering against the sky. You'll hear another note in a minute—faint and far and clear, like the other one, and sweeter still, you'll notice. Wait ... listen. There it goes! It says, *'It is I, Soldier—come!'* ...

"Now then, watch me leave a blue streak behind!"